KING SLAYER

A FOG CITY NOVEL

LAYLA REYNE

ABOUT THIS BOOK

It wasn't all a lie.

Christopher "Dante" Perri had one goal: vengeance for his murdered partner.
But truth is rarely so black and white.
And assassin kings are rarely so addictive.
He can't get enough of Hawes Madigan.

But now that Hawes knows he's a fed, the new king wants nothing to do with him.

Chris aches to be near him, to help secure his throne and keep him safe.
Hard doing when Hawes is determined to put a bull's-eye on his back.
His bravery is as attractive as it is infuriating.

When Chris's desperation boils over, Hawes finally lets down his guard.

But behind his walls lies a terrible secret.
Once learned, Chris will stop at nothing to destroy the king
who stole his heart and more.

*Twists and turns—and cliffhangers—continue in book two of
Hawes and Chris's M/M romantic suspense trilogy. Read at your
own risk!*

To Erin,
without whom Chris would probably still be badge-less.

ONE

Never fall for a mark.

Undercover 101. Hell, avid reader 101. As many assignments as Chris had worked, as many books as he'd read, he fucking knew better. He should've recognized the signs and thrown up a wall sooner.

Would it have mattered?

Looking down at Hawes Madigan, naked and handcuffed to the headboard—his trim, hard body coiled for a fight, his blue eyes liquid fire, his cock still half-hard, and his sharp mind no doubt working overtime—Chris figured probably not. No amount of training, no amount of reading, no amount of proper carriage, hair ties, or weaponry would change the fact that the place he most wanted to be right then was in that bed—with the enemy.

With the Prince of Killers.

No, the king.

Fuck.

Chris blinked away the frustrating hunger, blanked his face, and banked his futile desire. It didn't matter what he wanted. What mattered was the badge lying open on Hawes's chest and Chris's mission. The mission he'd spent three years preparing for and that had led him here.

His last mission.

The one that had come to a head yesterday and now required him to blow his own cover before someone else did.

"Your partner?" Hawes said, his voice a disbelieving whisper.

"Special Agent Isabella Constantine."

"Isabella. Constantine." Hawes repeated Izzy's first and last name slowly, as if wrapping his brain around the differences between fiction and reality. They were subtle—the first names so close, like Perri and Perry; Izzy's last name an Americanized version of her family's Greek one.

She had taught Chris that lesson early on in his ATF career. Construct a cover close to reality—name, occupation, history. Less likely to make an undercover slip, more likely to fool a doubting target. She had been a good agent. The best mentor and partner Chris could have asked for. Bringing her killer to justice was no less than the person who'd saved his life deserved. And the key to doing just that was currently at Chris's mercy. He'd never get a better shot, a more captive audience.

"You're going to help me find her killer," Chris said as he stepped toward the bed.

Hawes's gaze shot to his, clashing and sparking with incredulity. He laughed out loud—the same harsh, bitter sound that had scraped over Chris's bones the night they'd first met. "Are you insane? You're a fucking fed."

"Since when do you have a problem working with a badge? Braxton Kane is the chief of police."

Hawes's chilly laughter waned, as did the color in his hollow cheeks. "Did he know who you really were?"

"No."

Hawes held his gaze, judging the truth of Chris's answer. "I trust Brax," he said after a long moment. "I don't trust you." Emphasizing the point, he yanked again at the cuff around his wrist, the other metal end battering the rail where Chris had attached it.

Chris wrapped his free hand over Hawes's cuffed one and waited for Hawes to still. "You trusted me up until five minutes ago."

"Five minutes ago, I thought I knew who you were." Hawes arched and twisted his torso, casting the badge off his body and onto the opposite side of the bed from Chris. "Lies, all of it."

Gun trained on Hawes's lower half, deterring any kicks or sudden movements, Chris released Hawes's wrist and stretched over him to retrieve his badge. He pocketed it but remained leaning over Hawes, nose to nose. "Not everything."

Facts that were close to the truth, as Izzy had taught him, and emotional truths too, no matter how much Chris wished otherwise. Lies would make his job a hell of a lot easier, would make being done with this a whole lot less complicated.

Heat, doubt, and hope flared in Hawes's eyes, and the tension drained out of him—chin lowering, chest collapsing, spine hitting the mattress. An opening Chris's heart rate ratcheted up to accept. Only to have the door slammed in his face. Elbow locked, wrist flexed, Hawes swung his left arm up and aimed the jutting heel of his hand directly at Chris's temple.

Concussion incoming.

Chris batted down the attack and reared back, out of Hawes's reach, fighting the magnetic pull that had sprung up so quickly between them.

Hawes was clearly doing a better job of resisting the pull than he was. Tender emotions wiped from his eyes, they burned with anger, hate, and betrayal. "I'm not fucking helping you."

Well, if that's how he wanted to play things… Chris straightened, squared his shoulders, and kept his pistol at the ready, not trusting the assassin. "I have you on murder."

"I have the same on you."

"Self-defense in the act of an investigation."

"And mine wasn't?"

Chris couldn't argue that. Jodie would have killed Hawes. He'd acted to defend himself, more so than Chris had in killing Ray. But Jodie wasn't Hawes's only kill. "Lucas."

Hawes smirked. "Lucas disappeared."

It was Chris's turn to laugh. "Into the Bay, on your orders."

"I gave no such order. You were there."

"Explosives trafficking," Chris countered.

"You know I'm trying to get out of that business."

"But you're not out yet, are you? You manufactured and, until yesterday, were in possession of illegal explosives, which you'd planned to smuggle to a new owner under the guise of a real estate sale. Did I get that right?"

Hawes bit his bottom lip, as if struggling to hold in a string of fiery curses. The dam didn't hold long. "Fine, haul me in," he exploded. "I'm still not fucking helping you. I've done enough damage already. I'm not going to make it worse. Fuck, I'll be lucky if Holt and Helena ever forgive me as it is."

Chris lowered the hammer. "Funny you should mention them. You know what'll make things worse? The backup of Amelia's flash drive. She told me where it was before you and Helena stormed in. I get a hold of that, and I'll have everything I need to arrest you and your siblings."

As expected, Hawes froze, his struggle with the handcuff forgotten, Chris's threat to the people who mattered most to him capturing all his attention.

"You might not care about yourself, Madigan, but I know your weakness. That soul you can't hide. The one that'll do anything to protect your family, even if they aren't exactly innocent either."

Hawes gulped and slowly cast his gaze down, eyeing Chris's gun. Chris could swear he heard the brush of long lashes against pale cheeks. And again on the way back up.

But that was impossible... *Fuck!*

Realizing his mistake too late—that the faint, wispy sound had come from behind him—Chris shifted to defend himself. And in the next instant he was defenseless, the gun knocked from his grasp by a bare foot.

"And we'll do anything to protect him," Helena declared.

Chris spun her direction with a, "How the fuck—" but was cut off by Hawes's, "Low, Hena!"

She instantly dropped into a crouch. Metal clanked against wood behind Chris, and he whipped back around. Too late. Abs curled, Hawes was levering onto his shoulders and scissor-kicking his legs into the air. Not at Chris. At the exposed pipe hanging from the ceiling above the bed. Lofted as the bedroom was, Hawes had no problem reaching the pipe with his long legs, locking his heels around it, and—

Fuck!

Chris caught a face full of water, the dislodged pipe acting as a high-pressure hose. Spluttering, he raised a hand to protect his eyes and sidestepped the geyser. The crack of splintering wood had Chris dropping his hand and flinging off water, desperate to get clear eyes on the situation. Too late again. Hawes flung away the broken headboard rail dangling from the handcuff and vaulted onto his knees, while Chris fell to his, kicked from behind by Helena. He couldn't catch his breath, much less make a move to get ahead of them, their coordination practiced and deadly.

Helena cinched his wrists behind his back with a zip tie, then shoved him facedown onto the mattress. She scaled his back, light as a feather, lethal as a viper, then planted one foot on the mattress and the other on his nape. "Tell me right now why I shouldn't break your neck."

Chris ignored the instinct to fight and forced himself to still. Grappling with Hawes was a well-matched challenge. Add Helena to the mix, take away Chris's weapon, and it was a no-win situation, no matter how good he was at hand-to-hand combat. He had to be smart, had to use what he'd learned about the Madigans, and offer them something they couldn't refuse.

"I wasn't lying about the flash drive," he said.

"We'll find it," Helena replied, then told someone on the other end of a comm unit, "Kill the water." Holt, Chris assumed, had to be somewhere in the building in order to manually shut off the pipes.

"Maybe you'll find it," Chris said, once the geyser

quieted. His next words were aimed at Hawes, wherever he'd slid off the bed to. "And killing me is against your rules."

Helena pressed harder on his neck. "You're a threat."

"Who is after the same thing you are."

"Let him go, Hena."

She backed off with a gasp. "Hawes!"

Righting himself, Chris glanced across the room in the direction of Hawes's voice, and immediately understood Helena's change of tone. Hawes stood in the far corner, sheet wrapped around his waist, Chris's gun in his hand.

Chris stayed on his knees, intentionally at a disadvantage. Not a threat. "You won't use that."

Hawes lifted his arm and aimed the gun at Chris's head. No tremble, no hesitation. "Right now, you don't know what I'll do."

"Big H…"

The quiver in Helena's voice, together with Hawes's dark words and steady grip, were indication enough that Hawes was close to stepping over his self-imposed redline. One Chris respected. Pulling that trigger was the last thing Chris wanted to goad Hawes into doing.

"I'll go." Chris rested back on his heels, eyes downcast, chin lowered. He'd put his hands up too, if he could. "But my offer—"

"Didn't sound like an offer to me."

Lifting his head, Chris locked eyes with Hawes. "You need to know who is trying to unseat you. I need to know who killed my partner. We've worked well together the past week. We can solve this too."

"Get out, Agent Perri." Flat. Cold. Deadly. Not a trace of warmth or any other emotion.

Chris rose to his feet, and Helena perp-walked him down the stairs to the door, where she cut the zip tie with her knife. Chris held out a hand to Hawes, who stood behind her. "My gun?"

"No," Hawes said. "I think I'll keep it. Might come in handy."

Chris hoped like hell it didn't, almost as much as he hoped like hell Hawes stuck to his rules. Otherwise, there'd be no way out of this for any of them.

Chris swung into the South Park loop and found a spot in the line of cars parked along the curb, backing the Hog in behind a hideously flashy Maserati. He killed the engine, dismounted, and rifled through the books and detritus in his saddlebag for his earbuds. South Park was only two blocks from Hawes's condo; he couldn't have missed much.

Earbuds in, he opened the surveillance app on his phone and waited for the signal to connect. He kept his gait casual as he strode toward one of the perimeter benches in the bustling neighborhood park. As many times as he'd parked here the past week, the residents probably thought he was a new employee at one of the start-ups that rented space around the oval. Just another tech bro on his phone, nothing to see here, even if he did look half-drowned.

The static in his ears resolved, and Chris lowered himself onto the nearest bench, listening intently.

"Condo is clean," Holt said, confirming Chris's suspicion that Hawes's twin had been on-site. Not directly in the line of fire—all three Madigan siblings rarely were, especially if Holt had his daughter with him—but nearby to help control variables and get there quickly for the debrief. "No devices I can find."

Chris smiled. His supposedly undetectable tech was so far undetectable. Good. That said, given the bug's location, the volume of the voices inside the condo fluctuated depending on its carrier's proximity to the speaker. For now, it remained close enough to clearly transmit their conversation.

"I told—" Helena started.

"Don't need to hear it," Hawes said. "Already thought it myself. What led you here?"

A *thump* echoed through the comm, something solid landing on a table or the kitchen island. Chris had to kick up the volume on his device, the voices farther from his bug, the carrier likely scared off by the noise.

"You got the yearbook," Hawes said.

"And a lead on who was paying him." Holt paused to shush Lily, who, judging by her cries, also hadn't liked the sudden noise. Couch cushions groaned, and then a flurry of keystrokes followed. "When I couldn't find Perry with a *Y*, I searched variations."

"And found Perri with an *I*," Helena said. "The hard copy of the yearbook confirmed it."

"And his bank accounts are at a federal credit union," Holt said.

Chris pictured the giant man sitting on the couch, daughter strapped in the sling against his chest, laptop open on his knees, reaching around Lily to point to evidence on-screen that would confirm what Chris had told Hawes.

"Because he's ATF," Hawes said. "Saw the badge myself."

"We figured he was a fed. Guessed ATF, but we weren't sure."

"Regardless," Helena said, "I got here as fast as I could."

"Thank you for the save," Hawes replied.

"You would have rescued yourself, eventually." The smirk in her voice didn't last long. "Given our businesses and past investigations, ATF made the most sense."

"Wait, rewind," Holt interrupted. "How does *Christopher* translate to *Dante*? There are no references in the yearbook to him as Dante, even as a nickname. Was it just a cover?"

"No way," Helena said. "He responded to it naturally, and it's pressed on his card case."

Chris patted his coat pocket, panicked for a second that the leather bifold had fallen out when Helena had thrown his coat out after him. He released his breath when he found it secure in the inner pocket where he always kept it. Izzy had given it to him as a graduation gift when he'd completed Special Agent Basic Training. She'd had *Dante* pressed into one side. After her murder, he'd had her time of death pressed into the other. A reminder of his mission.

"Not just a cover," Hawes said, filling his siblings in on the same. "His work partner gave him the nickname."

"Partner?" Helena said. "At the ATF? Who's he work with?"

"Work*ed* with, past tense. His partner was Special Agent Isabella Constantine." As before, Hawes emphasized the last *A* of Izzy's first name and every syllable of her surname. "Or as we knew her, Isabelle Costa."

Holt and Helena inhaled sharply, and Lily wailed an angry punctuation.

"She called him Dante," Hawes explained, "because his nose was always stuck in a book."

While Helena muttered an impressive string of curses, Holt resumed his furious typing. With new search parameters, he'd find where Chris's and Izzy's paths had crossed in no time.

Unlike his siblings, Hawes was silent. No words, no pacing footsteps, no whisky bottles clinking against each other. Where was he? Leaning against the kitchen island or one of the condo's wooden pillars? Or was he standing in front of the balcony windows, arms draped over the metal seismic strut? Like he had been that first night Chris had sweet-talked his way inside the condo. Chris had tried to sweet-talk Hawes into more than just an invitation to enter. He hadn't set out to seduce the prince that night, but when the opportunity had presented itself, he'd considered it an inroad to the information he needed.

What Chris hadn't needed were the sparks that had flown between him and Hawes, the heat that had drawn him like a missile to his mark. He'd nuzzled behind Hawes's ear, inhaled the subtle scent of expensive after-shave mixed with dangerous man, and he'd been the one seduced. Add to that Hawes's humor and honesty, the curious glimpses of vulnerability, and the barest hint of submission, and Chris had actually wanted to help him, which was the last thing he'd needed.

This was supposed to be his final mission, and not because he'd gotten fired for falling for the mark, at least not yet. He couldn't let that happen, couldn't let that be the way this all ended. Get vengeance for his partner, then get out. That was the plan. He was shit at the ATF political game—that had been Izzy's thing, not his—and there was nowhere left for him to go in the agency that was as good a fit as undercover work. Except he was tired of being other people. After ten years of UC work, he needed to figure out who he was and where home was, for real. But, fuck if 'Dante' and Hawes's condo hadn't felt awfully close to real the past week, which only made the light at the end of his escape tunnel harder to see, diffuse and refracted like the fog Hawes loved so much.

"How's Rose today?" Hawes's question about his grandmother brought Chris out of his head and back to the present.

"Improving," Holt answered. "She'll be discharged tomorrow."

"You're not actually considering working with the fed, are you?" Helena persisted. "The risks if he finds out—"

"I know," Hawes snapped. "He can't."

Can't find out what?

Chris had no delusions about being fully read in. He'd known the Madigans were keeping secrets from him. They were too smart to tell him—a relative stranger—everything. He was outside their inner circle, even further now. And further still from whatever this thing was that affected him and the organization. It had to be about Isabella. Or the explosives. Or both. Chris was almost certain the two were tied together. What was it about that night that had pushed Hawes to make such radical changes in the organization? What exactly did Hawes know?

"We can't trust him," Helena said. "If that's not clear after today…"

"No argument here," Hawes replied. "But do we need him? I started the week getting close to a source, working him for information on who was moving against us. Can we still use him as such?"

Acid churned in Chris's gut. While neither of them had hidden the fact that they were using the other, hearing point-blank he'd gotten played was a kick in the balls. Was that all Hawes had been doing? Playing him? Had it all been a lie on his end, no matter how real it had felt to Chris? He didn't think so, given the betrayal in Hawes's eyes this morning and the heat in them last night, but Chris couldn't be sure, and he couldn't hang his hat on the 'started the week' qualifier in Hawes's statement. Not that Hawes's intentions, then or now, fucking mattered.

All that mattered was the mission.

Hawes again seemed to get that better than Chris, asking, "Can we use him and his resources to find out who is behind the coup against us?" When met with silence, Hawes barked, "Holt!"

"Huh?" Holt said, likely lost in computer code. "Sorry."

"I said, do we need Agent Perri's resources?"

"Let me see what I can do first."

"When's the last time you slept?"

Or the hacker had dozed off before and he didn't like being called out on it. "Broken record much?"

Hawes ignored the retort and shifted the conversation. "We need to find out where that flash drive backup is and get to it before Perri, if, in fact, he knows where it is."

"You think he's bluffing?" Helena asked.

"Yes." Good call. Apparently, Chris had shown Hawes more than a few of his moves too. "Have you been back to see Amelia?"

"Not yet," Helena said. "Holt?"

"I can't. And now with this..." His pained voice,

brought on by the mention of his wife, made Chris wince. "Did Brax know who he was? Who he worked for?"

"Dante—" Hawes paused, cleared his throat, then corrected. "Chris said he didn't."

"I don't think Brax would betray us," Helena said.

"I don't either," Hawes concurred, "but the only people we can completely trust now are in this room."

They could trust Kane, and Chris needed the chief to trust him too. As tightly allied as he was with the Madigans, Kane was the best positioned to serve as an intermediary. And Chris needed one because Hawes was right. They could still use each other—Hawes to find out who was behind the coup, Chris to find out who killed Isabella. Each had information the other needed, and Kane could broker that exchange. But if Chris had a shot in hell of getting Kane on board, of securing the flow of information, he had to be the one to tell Kane the truth before anyone else did.

And time was tight. Chris's boss had filled his voice mail overnight with warnings of her imminent arrival. He needed to beat her there. He pushed off the bench and hustled back to the Hog. Next stop, SFPD headquarters.

TWO

Chris was halfway across the bullpen floor before he considered that Kane might not be here today after their long night that had bled into morning. Chris dismissed the absurd thought as quickly as it had formed. Kane was up to his eyeballs in this shit, same as him. Given all that had transpired, Chris would lay odds on Kane being in one of three places—here at the station, at the Madigan family fort in Pacific Heights, or at the waterfront headquarters of Madigan Cold Storage. Since Chris would likely get shot if he visited either of the latter two, he prayed Kane was here instead.

Half the staff was out for lunch, but the remaining officers, each a pair of trained eyes, tracked Chris as he wove through the rows of desks. Maybe he was just as likely to get shot here. Had news of his blown cover leaked already? Had the Madigans alerted other allies on the force? Chris was sure Kane wasn't the only SFPD officer in their pocket. Or had someone on the force—Kane, perhaps—pieced together why he'd been lurking the past week, asking questions about a three-year-old investigation?

Or none of the above.

He turned the corner and a familiar voice echoed from inside Kane's office. "You should have called this in earlier, regardless of Agent Perri's actions. Given the explosives involved and previous investigations, this matter is squarely within the ATF's jurisdiction. It's our case now. Officially."

Fuck.

So much for telling Kane the truth first and salvaging some sort of working relationship. Vivienne Tran had beaten him here, and by the sound of it, she was approaching things in her usual incendiary manner. He sucked in a deep breath, readying to enter, then paused to do a quick pat down. Hair pulled back, shoulders squared, gun holst—

Fuck!

Tran would spot the empty holster, and when he'd have to confess it was in the hands of their target—an assassin— the dressing-down would be epic. Maybe epic enough to yank him from the case altogether, which he couldn't let happen. He unclipped the holster and searched for a place to stash it, trying the conference room door across the hall.

Locked.

Fuck, fuck, fuck!

"You need some help?"

Chris spun toward the voice and had to stop himself from laughing. The rubber-ducky-printed tie around the person's neck was the first welcome bit of hilarity today. The humorous tie was in direct contrast to the pressed khakis and starched dress shirt but made a certain amount of sense with the platinum Mohawk and gumball ear gauges. The person's dangling ID badge read: *Jax Dillon, SFPD IT,* and handwritten in marker in one corner: *They/Them.*

Chris hadn't seen them around the station before, but the laptop they carried had an SFPD sticker and barcode on it. Part-time intern, perhaps, or an employee just back from vacation. In any event, they didn't seem to know who he was. Good. Chris could use that.

"I do, actually." He held out the empty holster. "Can you hold this for me?"

Jax glanced at the leather case, then back to him, brow cocked above a skeptical green eye. "Why?"

"'Cause I asked nicely."

"I don't even know who you are."

Chris dug out his badge and flashed it open. "Special Agent Christopher Perri. ATF."

They thrust out a hip and shrugged, unimpressed.

Chris failed to hold in his laughter this time. All right, bribery it was, then. "You know Angelica's Bakery in North Beach?"

"Everyone knows AB's."

Local, if they knew to call it by the neighborhood shorthand. "You hold this for me"—he extended the holster again—"and I'll get you a box of mistletoe cannoli."

"But it's July."

And AB's mistletoe cannoli were only available one week a year, between Christmas and New Year's. Unless you were family. "Angelica's my cousin. I'll get—"

Jax snatched the holster out of his hand. "I'm in IT. Other side of the floor." They tucked the holster between the computer and their chest, turned on their heel, and strode toward the stairwell.

Chris was still smiling as he rapped his knuckles on Kane's door.

"Come in!" the chief shouted. Chris pushed open the door, and hard hazel eyes shot to his, killing Chris's lingering grin. "*Agent* Perri, I understand."

"Perri," Tran said, and Chris swung his gaze to the woman seated in the guest chair. One suited leg crossed over the other, dark hair in a tight bun, face calm, and black eyes flat, she was the picture of serenity. No hint that she had been flexing her jurisdictional muscle and vocal cords a second ago. "Was there a reason you didn't identify yourself to the chief of police in the jurisdiction where you were conducting an operation?"

Kane appeared equal parts furious and fearful. The former on behalf of those he considered family, the latter over whether that fact would be exposed. Brax knew exactly why Chris hadn't identified himself to him.

Time to tap-dance and win back some of that trust he needed. "Given the irregularities of the prior investigations," Chris said, "I thought it best to maintain full cover."

"Chief Kane wasn't involved in those prior investigations. He was only recently appointed chief."

"Ma'am—"

"You didn't think local law enforcement needed to know the ATF was pursuing an explosives trafficking lead in their backyard?"

"Explosives trafficking?" Still standing, Kane braced his hands on the desk, knuckles white where they curled around the edge. "I thought you were helping—" A sharp shake of Chris's head, and Kane adjusted. "I thought you were helping out on a missing person's case, *as a private investigator.*"

"The private investigator part was his cover," Tran said to Kane before redirecting her attention to Chris. "The other part was not your assignment. Is that why you haven't logged status reports in over a month?"

"Deep cover."

"Oh, cut the crap, Perri." She pushed to her feet. "You've gone rogue—*again*—after being repeatedly told to drop this."

"Drop what?" Kane asked.

"The investigation into Special Agent Isabella Constantine's death."

Kane's eyes widened, round as saucers. "As in Isabelle Costa?"

"Constantine," Chris corrected.

"Isabelle was ATF?"

"Isabell*a* was my partner. She was murdered, and she deserves justice."

Blanching, Kane bowed his back and hung his head between his outstretched arms. Before Chris could say more, Tran stepped between them. At five foot nine, closer to six feet in heels, she commanded his attention. "Agent Constantine's murderer was killed at the scene. That case was closed."

Chris scoffed. "Without a thorough investigation."

"Because doing so would have compromised the agency's mission, *her* mission, which you are here to complete. That's your assignment, Agent Perri. To get a lock on the explosives, secure them before they fall into even worse hands, and shut down the Madigans. Not go dark— off mission—like your partner also did."

Silence hung heavy in the office until it was cut by the groan of abused chair springs as Kane lowered himself into the leather swivel behind his desk.

"Status report, Agent Perri," Tran demanded.

"The person who last moved the explosives is behind bars." He flicked a hand in the air. "In this building still, I think."

"She is," Kane confirmed.

Not good enough for Tran. "And where are the explosives?"

Silence blanketed them once more. Chris didn't have an answer.

Tran glanced over her shoulder at Kane. He didn't have one either. But she had one for them. "Agent Wheeler will be here on Monday."

Chris bit back a groan, sure it would be louder than the chair springs if it escaped. Scotty Wheeler was a fucking by-the-book menace. Tran's pet UC wrangler. No undercover agent wanted to hear his name near their case. It was as good as getting a case ripped away.

"Respectfully, ma'am, I don't need a babysitter. And my cover—"

"Is shot to hell, judging by the events of the past twenty-four hours and by this bullshit exchange the past five minutes. You went rogue, it backfired, and now you're scrambling."

And that right there was how Vivienne Tran had climbed the ATF political ladder. She'd spot your weakness, what you were trying to hide, and use it to her advantage. A scorched-earth approach, and she was the last one standing with the blowtorch. Chris bet her favorite movie was *Aliens*.

"Your case is imploding, Agent Perri. The window for success is closing fast. You need help if the agency is going to secure the explosives and arrest the targets before they flee."

Kane flinched. Because Tran had referred to the Madigans—*plural*—as targets? Or at the notion they might flee? Chris wasn't sure how to read Kane, but he was sure about the Madigans, at least in one respect. "They won't flee," he told Tran. "Not with their power threatened, and not with—"

"Holt Madigan's wife, the mother of his child, in custody," Kane said, completing Chris's thought. "Holt won't leave."

"And Hawes and Helena won't leave without him," Chris added.

Tran stepped back and split her glare between them. "Good, but I'm still sending Wheeler in." She'd never intended otherwise. She grabbed her bag off the floor and headed for the door. "Get the explosives, Agent Perri. Shut down the Madigans. Do your job while you still have one."

The door slammed shut behind Tran, and Chris relaxed his shoulders, the tension draining from his posture. After a week of being Dante, he wasn't used to standing at attention, as one did when facing the agency firing squad, but he'd survived. He'd have an obnoxious, Scotty Wheeler-sized Band-Aid to show for it come Monday, but at least Tran hadn't pulled him off the investigation. Now he just had to survive the other firing squad. He turned to face

Kane, who'd risen as Tran had left. Chris lifted both hands, placatingly. "Brax, listen—"

"Don't." Fear gone, the chief's fury rumbled in his deep voice. Drawing himself up to his full height, Braxton Kane was an imposing figure. Granted, he was built more like a spindly pine than a redwood, but that flexible strength was probably what had helped him weather countless storms—army, Madigan, and otherwise. "You lied to all of us."

Chris sank into the chair Tran had vacated. He needed to refocus this conversation. Get back to his original purpose for coming here—to bring Kane around to his side, or, at a minimum, around to working with him. "You're law enforcement," he said. "You know how undercover works."

"I do." Kane crossed his arms, fingers digging into the wiry muscles of his sleeved biceps. "You're supposed to liaise with the local authorities."

"Except when those authorities are compromised." Chris had a guess as to what—or rather *who*—was Kane's Achilles' heel, but he didn't need to strike at that weak spot. Yet. "What would you have done if I'd told you who I really was? I didn't put you in that position because you're more valuable to me, and to them, if we're working together."

"Cruz vouched for you," Kane said.

"Because she knows the real reason I'm here."

"The explosives."

"Isabella."

Sighing, Kane released the death grip on his biceps and ambled over to the window. He skirted a hand over his short hair, then rested his forearm against the window frame, back to Chris. "Zander Rowe killed Isabelle Costa."

Not an attestation, more like a weary chorus. Same as the man himself.

"If you're half the cop I think you are, you know that's just as much a cover as my partner's name was."

Kane rotated and rested back against the window. "So Tran was right? You went rogue? Isabelle too?"

"Not rogue. Neither of us." Chris filched two candies out of the bowl on Kane's desk and tossed one to the chief. "Izzy went off the map a few days before her death. I still don't know why, but I think it has to do with those explosives and why she was killed. Which is my number one priority here."

"But not the ATF's."

"My priorities aren't ranked the same as the agency's."

"Oh, is that it?"

"I also knew there was a threat to Hawes."

Kane pitched the foil wrapper in the trash can and popped the candy into his mouth. "You used that to get close to him."

"Yes, until I realized what Hawes was trying to do." He clicked the hard candy against his teeth, recalling that morning in Hawes's bathroom. A double-edged sword—doubt and respect—had pierced his chest at learning Hawes was maneuvering the Madigans out of the explosives business. And then that blade had melted under the heat of something more when Hawes had turned down Chris's offered gun. He'd poured his conflicting emotions into the kisses he'd given Hawes that morning. All of it real in that moment. Same as Hawes's intentions for his family's empire. "They're not the same Madigans anymore, are they?"

Kane didn't reply. Smart, better not to let on how much he did or didn't know.

"They're moving away from high-risk, disreputable ventures," Chris continued. "And someone doesn't like that. Doesn't like Hawes."

"Amelia."

"Was working for someone else. The threat is still out there." He cast out a baited line, fishing. "To all of them."

Kane pushed off the window and returned to his desk. "So what do we do?"

And fish caught.

Chris pointed at himself. "*I* keep hunting Izzy's killer." Then gestured between them. "*We* work the explosives angle, which is connected to the attempted coup. The faction Amelia was working with and that wants to overthrow Hawes, stole those explosives. Finding the person behind the theft and the coup is in all our interests." He shifted forward and braced his elbows on his knees. "I need a meet before Wheeler arrives."

Kane spread his hands, palms up. "What makes you think they'll talk to me now?"

The defeat in Kane's voice sent a pang of regret rippling through Chris. He didn't like putting the chief in this position either. "I told Hawes you had nothing to do with it. That you didn't know who I was."

"But they know we'll be coordinating now."

"Then convince them we're still on their side." They'd believe Kane before they'd ever believed him.

"How do I know you are?"

"I could have turned them in at any point this week. I didn't."

"And why is that?"

"It's not in my interest to do so." Not when Hawes and his siblings could lead him to Isabella's killer. And not when his interest in Hawes had drifted beyond mark—beyond target—to something else, whether Chris had wanted it to or not.

"The bust you could make…"

"I don't care," Chris said. "I'm out after this case."

Kane's brows climbed to his hairline.

"I want Izzy's killer brought to justice, then I want to get on with living *my* life, or whatever's left of it."

"You want to come home."

"I do." He ignored the image that flashed behind his eyes—of Hawes in his bathroom—and stood, hand outstretched toward Kane. "Will you help me?"

The chief considered too long a moment, long enough to make Chris wonder whether he'd miscalculated in his approach, before he finally stood and shook Chris's hand. "This is my home too. I'm sworn to protect it." *And them,* he didn't have to say. "That's what I'll do."

THREE

Phone in hand, Chris glared at the dark screen. Over twenty-four hours and no word about a meet. He'd spent the day following leads on Amelia's flash drive. He'd bluffed about knowing its location. No luck finding it, at least in the places he could search. So he'd come here instead, to his mom's house, seeking distraction.

Which arrived right on cue. "Christopher?" His mother's voice echoed up from the downstairs garage. "Are you here?"

Chris dropped his phone back into his apron pocket and shouted over the footsteps trudging up the steps. "That's my bike down there, isn't it?" He'd left the door at the top of the stairs open, anticipating their arrival home from evening mass.

"Dad's bike," his sister said, appearing first through the door. "And it's missing an exhaust bolt."

Even with a living room and kitchen island between them, Celia's weary bitterness slammed into Chris. Three family dinners since he'd been back in town, and she'd been this way at each of them. He'd chalked it up to a mood the first time, had accepted her work excuse the second, but now a third time, and he figured he knew what was really up. But she'd bite his head off if he said a bad word about *him* in front of the kids, so he stuck to the topic at hand instead.

"Not the first time one of those has rattled off."

"And the helmet?"

"Left it in a hotel room somewhere."

"Uncle Dante!" Marco, his nephew, skirted around his mom. He half swaggered, half jogged across the living room, trying to play it cool but was hopelessly earnest. He held out a fist for a bump. "What's up?"

Chris formed a fist to bump back. "Lookin' sharp, Plato."

The nicknames had stuck since he'd first brought Izzy to one of their family dinners. Marco, then just a kid, had wanted one too, so Izzy had reached back into her heritage and picked a famous Greek philosopher.

With his other arm, Chris caught Marco in a playful chokehold and knuckled his head, messing up the dark curls he'd gelled into submission for Saturday mass. "Fuck, I'm too old for this shit," Marco protested.

"Language!" Celia chided as she hefted a tote bag onto the island. Her cuticles were wrecked, not just from caked on shop grease, and the bags under her eyes were more pronounced than last week.

Laughing to cover his scrutiny, Chris released his nephew and batted down his flailing right hook. "Maybe one day you'll land it."

Marco flipped him off, then snuck behind him to peer into the pot on the stove. "Butter chicken, yes!"

"Mia will be disappointed she missed it." Gloria, Chris's mother, joined Celia beside the island and added a bottle of wine to the bounty.

"Where is she?" Chris asked after his niece.

"Dinner with her boyfriend's family," Celia answered.

Marco rolled his eyes, hard, and Chris stifled another laugh as he unloaded the bag. "All I needed was cilantro," he said, ten other items later.

"And all I needed was cacciatore for dinner tomorrow night," Gloria quipped.

Chris chuckled. "Fair enough." He finally found the cilantro and set about picking off the leaves while his mother put the rest of her groceries away. "I'll call the shop tomorrow," he told his sister. "Set up a time to get the bike fixed." They, and before them, their father, had put in too much work to keep the classic Hog running. Chris wouldn't slack off now.

Celia jutted her chin at the stove. "How much time we got left?"

"Ten minutes or so. Just waiting on the rice."

"No need to call the shop. I have tools and bolts in my truck."

Before he could object, Celia was backtracking toward the garage, pulling up her cascade of dark curls as she went. She fumbled with the rubber band around her wrist once, twice, then let the hair fall back down, giving up the effort. More signs of her exhaustion, but gone were the days when they could talk about it, about anything really. Their relationship had changed, irrevocably, a decade ago. Not his choice then, but he hadn't pushed to repair it over the years and he'd all but abandoned it the past three. Had he missed his chance?

For now, he'd settle for providing the help she'd accept. He grabbed Marco by the shirt as he tried to sneak out of the kitchen. "Go help your ma."

He grumbled about being told what to do, not about the task itself. Like his mom and grandpa, Marco rarely passed up the chance to get his hands greasy. He wasn't legally old enough to work in the shop yet, but he was there every chance he got. Stripping down to his undershirt, he tossed his tie and dress shirt on the couch before disappearing down the stairs.

"You didn't want to come with us to mass?" Gloria asked.

He bent and kissed her cheek. "Wouldn't have made it in time."

"But you made it here in time to get dinner started?"

"Priorities," he confessed with a cheeky grin.

She swatted his shoulder, then dug the bottle opener out of a drawer. "Shut your mouth before St. Peter hears you."

"Pretty sure I'm already on the Do Not Admit list."

"Nonsense," his mother said. "You're a good boy." Chris laughed out loud, and she giggled along with him. She'd picked him up from detention enough times to know better. She spritzed the naan with water and tossed it into the preheated oven. "Now that brother-in-law of yours, he's not getting anywhere near the pearly gates."

Just as Chris had suspected. "Dex is gone again?"

"Hopefully for good."

Chris agreed, but they'd said the same thing the countless other times his sister's sorry excuse for a husband had decided family life wasn't a good fit for him. "What's the likelihood of that?"

"About as likely as you ever settling down."

"Ma…"

"I know." She picked up her glass and took a swallow of her favorite rosé. "With everything you've lost, it's easier to keep moving. I can't fault you for that." Disappointment tangled with compassion in her voice, and Chris ducked his chin to force down the lump in his throat.

UC work had kept him away except for random fly-bys, and even those had dwindled since Izzy's death. He missed his family—the humor, the food, the love—but being around them reminded Chris of the other things he missed—the life and future he'd lost. It was easier to ignore the painful losses when he was someplace else, someone else. Izzy had recognized that and steered him onto a new path, one where he could lose himself for weeks, months, on end. He'd be forever in her debt for that blessed courtesy.

But he couldn't run forever. Like Celia, he was exhausted, tired of running from his demons. And he wanted to be here for his family. But had he been gone too long to reclaim his spot? Was there a place for him here, for the person he was now? Or would be, when he figured out who the hell that was? He'd cooked and laughed with his family the last few weeks, but it wasn't the same. They thought he had one foot out the door, as usual. Truth be told, he hadn't fully committed to stepping over that threshold the other way either.

Gloria threw an arm around his waist. "I'm glad to have you back in town, for however long you can be here."

"Thanks, Ma." He kissed the top of her salt-and-pepper

head. Then took a first step. "I'm hoping it'll be longer this time."

"How much longer?"

Chris looked from his mother toward the voice, and his gaze clashed with Celia's dark, haunted one. She stood next to the couch, clutching Marco's dress shirt.

He took another step, most of the way over that threshold. "For good, I hope."

Gloria gasped, then clapped, while Celia white-knuckled her son's shirt. "You hope," his sister scoffed. She looked almost frightened yet sounded pissed he'd added the 'I hope' caveat. Did she want him back or not?

"Cee," Chris entreated, confused as fuck.

"*Your* bike is fixed." She spun on her heel and headed back toward the garage. "We're going to the store to grab soda." The garage door slammed shut behind her, cutting off any reply.

Gloria rested her weight against Chris's side. "It's been a rough week."

Chris laughed, both bitter and sympathetic.

The same dark eyes as his and Celia's stared up at him. "You too?" his mother asked.

"Oh yeah, me too."

"Butter chicken will fix that." She lifted her glass and swirled the pink contents. "So will wine."

"Pour me a big one, then."

Snickering, she poured him a tankard's worth, far more than was decent in any wine glass. "Are you really coming home?"

"Can I?"

"Always, Christopher." She handed him the glass and clinked the rim of her glass against his. "Well, not to this house, because I've earned my peace and quiet, and you have your own home, but you will always have a place in this family."

"Thanks, Ma." He gave her another peck on the head and smiled, covering the worry that still swirled over Celia's reaction, over what was going on in his sister's life. Worry that continued to mount as he put the final touches on dinner. Two sets of footsteps were on their way up the stairs, and Chris had just set the steaming plates of rice and butter chicken on the table, when the phone in his apron pocket vibrated. He pulled it out and read the text from Kane.

Gary Danko. Tomorrow night. 8:30.

Finally.

Except now that was another worry added to the mountain.

Chris drained what was left of his wine and helped himself to another too full glass, muffling his worry and the dangerous hope of home—not just with his family—that threatened to eclipse it.

Chris flipped the card case in his hand, end over end, in time with his bouncing thoughts and measured steps, back and forth across his study, working off dinner and working through ideas. He had a meet with Hawes tomorrow. Progress. He wanted more.

But two hours later, the temporary high of forward momentum had withered and died, leaving behind his old friend frustration. His constant companion the past three years.

Start from the top.

Izzy's voice rang in his head—consonants sharp, vowels long, all of it nasal. Her New York accent—Astoria, Queens —had been like nails on a chalkboard at first, grating and obnoxious. Now it was a comfort, if only in his imagination.

"Hawes Madigan," he said, speaking to a ghost. "King, head of the empire." Chris rested on the corner of his paper-strewn desk, which he'd crammed into the bay window nook in the front room of his condo. He glanced at the long wall to his right. It was covered with photos and colorful strings, arranged in a pyramid of sorts. He'd used his and Izzy's case notes, and the notes from the previous investigations, to construct a hierarchy of the Madigan organization.

The illegal one.

Helena and Holt were on either side of Hawes on the top line of the chart. Hawes didn't make an impact decision without discussing it with his siblings. He was the king as far as the outside world was concerned, but Chris knew his secret, confessed on a night when the crown had been too heavy to bear. Hawes didn't want to be king, not if he had to destroy his soul again to do it. It had been a devastating blow when sixteen-year-old Hawes had had to make the call to take his parents off life support. Then last week, he'd had to guide the family through his grandfather's passing. Hawes needed his siblings to step up and into equal roles in the organization's leadership apparatus if he was going to survive, regardless of who else was gunning for them.

On either side of the triumvirate—not a row down, but not quite on the same line—Chris had put the rest of the nuclear family: their grandmother, Rose; Holt's wife, Amelia; and Kane. Not related by blood or marriage, as far as the chief went, but he was family to them and vice versa.

The next line down listed the organization's lieutenants: Jodie, Ray, Lucas, Avery, Zoe, and Rowe. All of them, except Avery and Zoe, had red string X's over their pictures—deceased. Below them, captains Chris had heard mention of but hadn't laid eyes on. And below the captains were soldiers, some of whom Chris had seen at MCS. All in all, not an uncommon structure for a criminal enterprise. More complicated than the mafia but not unlike the cartel Chris had infiltrated in Florida or the gun-running motorcycle club he'd busted in Seattle.

Where does the next hit come from? Izzy prompted.

Chris ruled out Hawes's siblings. He'd mistakenly gone down that path before, wrongfully accusing Holt, and he had the mess on his hands now to show for it. He'd come around to Hawes's conviction: Holt and Helena wouldn't turn on their brother. Same as Chris would never turn on Celia. Nor on his mother. He ruled out Rose accordingly, and besides, she'd been in the car with Hawes when they'd been targeted after Papa Cal's funeral. Taking out the matriarch would have been another powerful blow to the family, possibly too devastating to come back from after just losing Cal.

Kane was a nonstarter. The chief had nothing to gain and everything to lose from a coup that would overthrow and threaten the trio. Avery had proved her loyalty. Zoe too. Which left…

"The captains."

Unless…

"An uprising among the soldiers."

But Chris doubted a lowly soldier was pulling Amelia's strings. She was too much of a force in her own right, too focused on power for herself and for Lily's legacy, albeit a different one than Holt and his siblings wanted for the munchkin. No, someone else with more juice had manipulated Amelia. They'd moved her around the board like they'd done with Jodie, Ray, and Lucas.

"An outsider," Chris reasoned. "Someone who'd promised Amelia the head of the table when this was all over. Someone who wanted an ally there and was willing to use those explosives to do it. Maybe for something else too." He picked up his tacks and string and put a red X out to the right side of the org chart.

Good, Dante. Now, when did the outsider enter the picture?

He rotated and examined the opposite wall.

Crime scene photos and reports from the night of Izzy's death were assembled in a collage with three years' worth of case notes. It had been the first thing Chris had arranged in his home office when he'd returned to San Francisco for this operation. He didn't care about the holes in the walls; they needed a fresh coat of paint anyway. He'd do that once he completed this mission, once he was done and had time to transform this place back into a home.

He reached out and grabbed the top folder off the stack on his desk. Withdrawing the offshore bank account ledger he'd shown to Hawes, he flipped it over to the oldest highlighted transaction on the back. He grabbed another tack and added this latest piece of evidence to the collection. Three years ago, Amelia had paid Zander Rowe from that account. Two years after Hawes had assumed the throne, operationally if not officially.

Their mysterious outsider was playing the long game. They'd decided fairly quickly that they didn't want Hawes in charge. Had made an attempt using Rowe somehow, and it had backfired. After Izzy's death, Hawes had solidified the organization's new direction. Gone even further toward caution and vigilantism versus straight-up fear and power. So the objectors, led by this outsider, had waited until Papa Cal's death—the official transfer of power—to strike.

Why, Dante?

"Because transfers of power are hectic. A good time to strike."

But that couldn't be all. He glanced out the bay windows on the other side of his desk. He couldn't see the Bay from here, but it was out there. And so too was Lucas, somewhere at the bottom of its inky depths. He remembered what the traitor had said on the boat that day Hawes had all but ordered him killed. Remembered what Amelia had said in her final stand at the condo. "Because someone thought Hawes was weak."

Hawes, however, had embraced the perceived weakness —in his person and his motives—and had made it his strength. And now he wasn't just a prince but a king. A threat of the highest order.

To whom?

"Competitors, former allies, former clients."

And who can lead you to those?

"Amelia Madigan."

Chris had been focused on digging into Hawes's connections, then into Holt's. Time to shift gears. Amelia was his way in. Who had she crossed paths with? Where did her loyalties truly lie? Were the answers on the flash drive backup? Where the fuck was it? He needed to find it before the Madigans did. And he needed to find the outsider before Hawes did, because, while it was in the ATF's and Chris's interests to catch that person and put them on trial, to get justice for Izzy's death, among other crimes, Hawes, Chris expected, had a very different endgame in mind. The only one that would secure his family's future and protect those he held dear.

You can't let that happen.

"I know."

Even if a not small part of Chris didn't object to Hawes's brand of justice.

FOUR

The light on the flash drive plugged into Chris's computer blinked orange, signaling the file transfer was in progress, just as the *click* of electronic door locks sounded from his desk speakers. He'd powered them on and synced them with his phone as soon as he'd returned home. Someone else had finally returned home too.

"Hey, girl," Hawes said. "Sorry I was gone all day." His voice was gentle and quiet—and tired, his exhale breathy, his syllables long. People claimed there wasn't a California accent, and Chris generally agreed, except there was a distinctive cadence, which was more noticeable when it was off, like it was in Hawes's voice now.

Iris let out a warbling *meow*, sounding both angry and confused. She made the noise again, then screeched a protest *yowl*. Hawes's words were amplified when he spoke next. "Just me, you little traitor."

Chris smiled at the memory of being stretched out on Hawes's couch, pretending to be asleep with Iris on his feet while Hawes prepared for a job, and at the irony of

Hawes's words, more true than he knew. Chris had tucked his bug into the narrow folds of Iris's collar, which was transmitting loud and clear with the cat in Hawes's arms.

"I still love you anyway," Hawes cooed. "Let's get you some food." His voice faded as he put Iris down, the cat no doubt scampering off to her bowl in the kitchen.

Chris turned the speaker volume down and tried not to listen too closely as Hawes moved about his condo. If Hawes contacted his siblings or another organization associate, Chris would detect the change in tone and tune back in. Until then, he didn't want to completely trample Hawes's expectation of privacy. The condo—*his home*—was a safe haven, from work, the organization, and his family, when he needed a break. As it was, it had been violated by the chaos Amelia had wrought. Chris didn't want to compound any insecurity Hawes already felt inside the space… which consideration for his mark was fucking ridiculous. Chris should be doing everything he could to throw Hawes Madigan off-balance, to make him feel unsafe and on-guard. He'd be more likely to make a mistake then, and Chris had an inside track. He knew better than most which buttons to push to multiply the mistakes. He'd made a physical and emotional connection with the cold, untouchable, beautiful, and efficient killer Izzy had described in her files. Chris didn't disagree with the latter two, but the first two couldn't be further from the truth. Everything about Hawes was hot, and every inch of him was eminently touchable. The waves of light brown hair, the smooth pale skin dotted with freckles, all those sharp angles. Chris had convinced himself that he'd been the one taking Hawes apart that night in the condo against the ladder, finding a way into the assassin's mind and body, but

Hawes had snuck under Chris's skin too. Further even, if the ache in his chest and groin were any indication.

Not good, Izzy chided.

"No shit, Sherlock."

He propped his elbows on the desk and scrubbed his hands over his face. Fingers tunneling into his hair, he loosened the tie around his topknot and massaged his scalp as the long strands fell free. This couldn't be about what he wanted. None of that mattered until he was done, *after* he found Izzy's killer and closed the ATF's investigation into the explosives. Chris had a better chance of succeeding on both fronts by working with the Madigans against whoever it was working against them. That was the real enemy here —the party who wanted to turn the organization back into the indiscriminate killing machine of Papa Cal's reign. The party who would use the stolen explosives to make their objective a reality. It was all twisted and tied together. Chris couldn't solve one without the other.

Which was what he needed to focus on. Not the *clink* of whisky bottles, not the *splash* of water in Hawes's shower, not the snippets of the Giants game on replay, and not Hawes's light snores. Not how rumpled and enticing Hawes must look lying on his couch. Like he'd looked Friday morning before Chris had woken him—wavy top strands sticking out in every direction, lean, corded muscles relaxed in sleep, a layer of darker scruff shadowing his angular jaw.

He wanted him still, maybe even more so than when he'd last seen Hawes. But what would be left of what he wanted when he was done with what he had to do? Was there a shot in hell Hawes would ever forgive him? That he'd ever touch—

Stop it!

His voice, not Izzy's. He shut down the thoughts making his jeans uncomfortable and got back to work. He took another spin through his and Izzy's files, recasting contacts and events around Amelia, searching for her connections and hiding places. An hour later, he was scrolling through search results—pre-Madigan-Amelia's last known addresses and places of employment cross-referenced against all persons flagged in the previous Madigan investigations—when Hawes's voice trickled out of the speakers again. Chris turned up the volume so he could hear it more clearly.

"No, no, no," Hawes mumbled. "Get off me! I can't just leave!"

Chris shot to his feet and snatched his keys off the desk. Someone was in Hawes's condo trying to force him to leave. Granted, Hawes could take care of himself, but if the intruder had surprised Hawes in his sleep, like Chris had done yesterday, then Hawes could be at their mercy. *Fuck,* Chris needed to get there. But he couldn't get there quickly enough from his place in Mission Dolores. He should alert Kane, get an officer on Hawes. Or better yet…

Chris grabbed his phone and scrolled to Holt's contact info. But then he stalled, thumb over the Call button, as his mind pushed through the panic to comprehend what he was hearing.

"No, no, no," Hawes repeated. "Get off me! I can't just leave!"

If an assailant was in the condo, if an actual fight was imminent, Iris would have bolted, not gotten closer, as indicated by Hawes's louder mumbles. Add to that her frantic purring, so loud it sounded like the hum of Chris's Harley, and he deduced the cat was trying to wake her owner from a nightmare.

Finally, she *meowed*, so plaintive and piercing that Chris winced.

And Hawes fell silent. Until the counting began. Same as it had the first night Chris had slept there, then again the night after Papa Cal died. Those times Chris had been in Hawes's condo. He could have gone to him if necessary. But Hawes had shaken himself out of it after a few repetitions, the arrival of his siblings hastening the process. Tonight, however, Hawes was alone, the counting continued, and Chris was halfway across town, feeling untethered, like Hawes had described feeling earlier in the week.

Chris tapped back to his contacts list, thumb hovering over Hawes's name. Would he even take Chris's call? In the unlikely event he did, what the fuck would Chris say? He had zero reason for calling at one in the morning. It wouldn't be case related. They already had a meet scheduled for that. No, this was dick related at best, heart related at worst.

"Fuck!"

Chris bolted out of the study and charged into the kitchen, nearly ripping the fridge door off in his haste to get a beer. He tossed the phone onto the island, dug out a bottle opener, and popped the cap, which bounced off the tiles and rolled across the hardwood floor toward the study. Tempting him to follow it back in there. To listen. He rounded the kitchen island and leaned back against it, pretending not to see the cap there, not to hear the only other sound in his too quiet condo.

Hawes's counting.

Through half the bottle of beer, then the rest of it.

Chris snatched up the phone and hit the Call button.

Iris hissed, knocked something over as she skittered across the metal coffee table, and Chris realized he only had a couple of seconds to move—the time it would take Hawes to reach for his phone—or else Hawes would hear the echo from Chris's speakers.

He hustled the length of the open kitchen, past the dining table, and down the long hallway bisecting his unit, to the seating area at the back of his narrow, second-floor condo. This area was intended as a mudroom entry from the stairs leading down to the backyard, but Chris rarely ventured out there. Instead, he'd made this room his reading nook—a leaning bookcase brimming over with paperbacks on one short wall, a coffee table and low-slung chaise on the long wall, and across from the chaise, big casement windows through which he had a decent view of the city. South, toward the condo and the man in it, who answered his call with, "It's late."

Better than the "fuck off" Chris had expected. He moved a stack of books from the chaise to the bookshelf, then lowered himself into the lounge's soft padded corner. "You're awake."

"So are you," Hawes said, rough and rumbly. "At one in the morning. Why's that?"

"Was reviewing Izzy's case files."

"Izzy." The background noise of the TV quieted. Still in the den, and by the lack of footsteps anywhere, still on the couch. "Your partner."

How much to disclose? Chris wanted to keep Hawes talking, keep him engaged, and this particular cat was out of the bag already. A little truth could go a long way. "I considered her that, as much as two undercover agents could be. She recruited and trained me at a time when I needed a new direction. One of us would be in the field, undercover, while the other was operational backup. Then, about four years ago, we were assigned separately. I was sent to Florida on a cartel sting."

Hawes was silent, long enough that Chris checked to make sure the call hadn't dropped. "Hawes, you there?"

"And she was sent to infiltrate my organization." His dark tone set off a ripple of goose bumps that lifted the hairs on Chris's arms.

"That's right."

"And three years later, here you are." Hawes hummed, contemplative. "Patience."

"Something like that."

Pensive gave way to indignant. "You waited until I was weakest."

"No." Chris shifted forward on the chaise, as if to emphasize his point to an imaginary Hawes leaning against the windows. "I waited until I got that flash drive and it became apparent someone else was making a move."

"So that wasn't bullshit?"

"I told you it wasn't all a lie."

"It's hard to sort out what was and wasn't."

"Ask me." The truth had kept Hawes talking so far. Chris could offer him more, anything, to reestablish this connection. For the sake of the case, of course, nothing to do with what he wanted.

"Are you really from here?" Hawes asked.

Chris bit back his sigh of relief and settled in for the conversation he'd wanted all day. Lifting and bending one leg, he rested it on the cushions and slung an arm along the back of the chaise. "Yes, born and raised in North Beach."

"Is your family still here?"

"They are."

Hawes huffed in disbelief. "Why would you tell me that? You're putting them at risk."

"I'm not." Of that, Chris was sure, more so with Hawes's organization than with any other he'd investigated. "Hurting them would be against your rules."

"My rules…" Hawes's words died on a bitter chuckle.

It scraped over Chris's bones, same as it had earlier. He hated it, hated the doubt he'd added to that mix. "Your rules are a good thing, Madigan."

"Should have recognized that for what it was. *Cop.*"

"Why didn't you?"

"I considered it when you walked into Danko." The leather of the couch creaked and fabric shifted, Hawes relaxing more on his end too. "But then Brax didn't know you, and…"

"And what?"

"That hair."

Chris's cheeks heated, recalling how often Hawes's gaze had strayed to the long strands, how his hands had tunneled through it, how he'd curled a hank around his fist and tugged. Chris had nearly come on the spot. "You like the hair."

"Too fucking much." Judging by the gravel in Hawes's voice, his mind had gone to the same place. "That, plus your *Madigans.* Sexy."

Chris dropped his arm off the back of the chaise, hand landing on his thigh. "Street ran both ways, with your *Mr. Perrys.*"

"So the formalities wouldn't have done me any favors, *Mr. Perry?*"

"Christ." Chris scooted down and spread his legs, trying to make more room for his thickening cock. "No, *Madigan*, they would not."

This was not the conversation Chris had anticipated tonight. He'd needed to get closer again, for the case, but this... This was the closer he wanted but didn't need. And he was powerless to stop it. Just like he was powerless to stop from sliding his hand toward his erection, which was pressing against the back of his zipper, demanding attention. He gripped himself through the denim, intending to stave off the building desire. He stroked down his length instead. "Probably would have fucked you sooner," he gritted out. "Taken you on that deserted dock if you hadn't stormed off."

Hawes had been glorious. Fitted, navy suit pants that showed off his high and tight ass, light-brown hair fog kissed and windswept from the ride on the yacht, blue eyes that burned bright with power and lust. Chris bet those eyes were burning bright again now.

Another stroke and Chris bit his lip to hold in the groan.

"I would have let you," Hawes replied raggedly. "Was already hard."

"Like you are now?"

"Fuck, Dante."

Chris bobbled the phone and had to interrupt another stroke to save the device from crashing to the floor. Recovered, he put the phone on speaker and set it on the arm of the chaise. He needed both hands to get his fly open and his dick out as fast as he could. "I remember how you tasted later that night," he said. "Like the fog." He swiped his fingers over the slit, collecting moisture, and spread it down his cock, slicking his grip. He closed his eyes and dropped his head back onto the chaise's arm. "Light and dark," he said, remembering the moment. "Hidden and open." Reliving it. "Suffocating, then freed."

"I can't," Hawes gasped.

Chris paused his strokes and rolled his face toward the phone. "Say the word, and I'll hang up."

"Too late."

Yes, it was, on so many levels. And on this one, Chris wasn't going to pump the brakes any more than Hawes was. "Get your dick out of those track pants," he said, figuring that's what Hawes had changed into after his shower. Commando, as he was prone to do. "And pull your shirt up." He closed his eyes again, imagining the sight. Hawes laid out on his couch, track pants bunched around his thighs, ribbed tank rucked under his chin, bared torso clenched with tension, the pale skin blotched red with rising heat as Hawes's hand shuttled up and down his cock.

Chris pushed his own jeans down farther, stripped off his shirt, and stroked himself faster. "Let me help you," he urged. "Let go for me."

"Look where that got me. You lied. You betrayed me. I should fucking hate you." The smart, rational part of Hawes's brain was fighting him, even as precome made his strokes audible, even as his breaths between words grew short and choppy.

"You liked being under me."

"Fuck, too much." Hawes groaned, wanton and needy, and Chris had to squeeze his balls to stave off his charging orgasm.

"I liked it too. All that straining muscle, all that strength matching my own. Your hands digging into my biceps. Holding on for dear life."

"Oh God." Hawes panted, breaths uneven, his words stuttered. "Too good. Too close."

"No such thing," Chris said, right there with him. He wished like hell he could see Hawes, wished he was there with him. But they could get somewhere else together. "Get there, Madigan."

Hawes's groan was long and broken, and on it, a wrecked, "Dante."

Chris tumbled over the edge with him, streaks of come splattering his torso as pleasure, desire, and desperation erupted in a blinding orgasm.

They caught their breaths in rhythm, together still, and Chris was the first to speak. "Wish that had been my mouth on you again."

"That jock and cheerleader really didn't appreciate what they had."

"You've seen the yearbook now. No better in print and no better in real life then either."

Chris's chuckle was met with dead silence on the other end of the line. A beat later, Chris realized the mistake his lust-fogged brain—and mouth—had made.

"How'd you know that?" Hawes asked, his voice a dangerous whip. Fully alert, all trace of their shared pleasure gone.

"I assumed," Chris tried to cover. "Holt said he was retrieving it."

"Or my condo is bugged."

"I assume you swept for bugs."

"You assume." Hawes's quick, determined tread echoed over the line. He was on his feet, moving around the condo. "Your assumptions and your plans, Mr. Perri. I can't trust any of them. Lesson learned." Ice cold, not the least bit of heat.

Chris fucking hated the freeze-out, especially after they'd just burned so hot together. After he'd managed to get close again. Dammit! He had to get back there, or at least try to. Trust—that was the key. That was where they kept getting tripped up.

He wiped off his torso with his shirt and stood, hiking up his pants. He hustled to the study and turned the speakers up, listening. "Give Iris a scratch for me," he said. "She's in your closet."

Hawes ended the call, and a moment later snuffed out the bug, a blast of static giving way to silence.

"It wasn't all a lie," Chris said to no one.

FIVE

Chris pushed open the restaurant's heavy glass door, and the wave of déjà vu almost made him stagger. The same hostess stood at her stand, Kane sat on a stool at the bar, and Hawes occupied the corner booth on the far side of the dining room. But that's where the similarities to last Sunday ended. No lively music played, no enticing aromas wafted from the kitchen, and no other diners filled the rest of the tables. The only patrons tonight were the king and two of his most loyal, most deadly allies, Helena and Avery.

The hostess stepped out from behind her stand and extended an arm toward Hawes's table. "Your party is waiting, Mr. Perri." Coat draped over her other arm, she sidestepped Chris and placed a set of keys on the bar next to Kane. "Anything else, Chief?"

Kane drew the keys toward him. "We're good, Ashleigh." Chris couldn't see Kane's face, but his bedraggled voice said plenty about the weekend he'd had. Worse than even Chris's. "Thank you."

"Just drop the keys in my mail slot before dawn." She squeezed his shoulder, flashed a smile at Hawes's table, then slipped out the front door, ignoring Chris completely.

He waited for the door to thunder shut behind her before sliding into the space next to Kane. "They bought the place out?"

"They don't trust you anymore." The chief rolled a cut-crystal tumbler between his palms, sloshing the two fingers of amber liquid inside the glass. Scotch, judging by the color and peaty smell tickling Chris's nose. "Don't trust me much either."

"And yet we're both here, and they haven't shot us."

Kane side-eyed him. "Yet."

Chris didn't doubt that Helena and Avery had their weapons within reach, if not drawn and trained on him beneath the table.

"Thanks for setting this up."

"You're lucky they answered my call." Kane drained his scotch and reached over the bar to place the glass in the sink. "And don't thank me yet." He straightened, wiped his hands, and slid off his stool. "Let's see how this goes first."

Kane led the way across the dining room rather than standing guard at the bar. He was joining them this time. As a mediator? Chris didn't dwell on the thought too long, his attention seized instead by the man seated at the middle of the table—the man whose lips were pressed into a thin line, whose posture was on guard, and whose blue eyes tracked his every step. Chris tried to take each step more like Dante, less like Special Agent Perri. Dante was the name Hawes had moaned last night when he'd come, the man he'd let in again. The man Chris had wanted to be more than anyone else for those too brief minutes, maybe who he wanted to be now more than a little—a lot after this was done. More than who he wanted to be, Dante was who Chris needed to be for this meet to pay off.

A meet he was lucky to have. After disclosing the location of the bug to Hawes, Chris had waited all day for the cancellation call to come. He'd taken a gamble, which could have gone either way. A final destruction of trust or an ounce of it earned. The phone never rang. Either he'd won back enough trust for Hawes to keep this meet, or this was a trap and he'd walked right into it.

Hawes's frigid "Mr. Perri" made Chris think the latter. No sexy rumble, no trace of warmth, no hint of a *Y* instead of an *I*. This was the cold, untouchable Hawes Madigan from Izzy's files. The only sign of emotion was the quiet, restrained anger that practically vibrated off him, as though his dark, fitted suit was the only thing keeping him contained. "I don't know what more we have to say to one another, but you requested this meeting"—he spread his hands—"so we're here."

Chris lowered himself into the chair next to Kane and nodded a greeting to Helena and Avery. Helena appeared aloof, while betrayal burned in Avery's dark eyes. Still loyal to her employers. Good. And of their missing party… "How's Holt?" Chris didn't expect him to be here if Hawes and Helena both were, but he probably wasn't far away.

Hawes's gaze flickered to Kane, a look passing between them. "Fine." Holt was anything but fine, if Chris had to guess from that terse response.

But before he could question further, Helena turned her I'm-barely-tolerating-your-presence glare on him. "Get on with it, Mr. Hair."

Chris chuckled, the tension-filled air around them lightening a smidgen. "We're sticking with that, then?"

"What else am I supposed to call you? Dantopher?"

And lightening a bit more. He held up his hands, palms out. "Things got out of hand Friday."

Stony silence. So much for the reprieve.

"We can still work together," he ventured.

"I don't see how that's possible." Hawes pointed a finger at him. "Fed." Then at himself. "Target of a federal investigation."

Chris jutted a thumb at Kane. "LEO. You work with him."

"Because we've known Brax for over a decade," Helena said. "He's proved he can be trusted." She tilted her head, long blonde hair cascading over her leather-clad shoulder. "You, not so much."

"Let me see if I can change that." He pulled back one side of his denim jacket, moving deliberately and obviously, and reached inside the inner pocket. He bypassed his leather card case and withdrew the flash drive he'd prepared last night. He pushed it across the table. "That's a copy of the file from the judge's desk." Not wanting to implicate them in front of Kane, Chris didn't mention Campbell by name, the target who'd given Hawes the tip on the current investigation right before Hawes and company had murdered him and set it up to look like a suicide.

Eyes flaring, Hawes accurately read between the lines. "So it was the ATF?"

Chris nodded. "Higher-ups got wind you were moving the explosives. Reopened the prior investigation."

"They thought they'd get us on the sale?"

Chris nodded again. "I convinced them I could infiltrate quickest."

Hawes traced his index finger around the rim of his glass. Chris thought he detected a tremble. "Because you thought you could seduce me." Or, given the barely contained fury in Hawes's voice, the assassin was readying to pick up the heavy cut crystal and throw it at him.

Chris backpedaled, fast. "Not part of my original plan."

Hawes rolled his eyes. "And we've come full circle, back to your *plans*."

Chris ignored the jab and made his case before objects started flying. "I had Isabella's files and knew them better than anyone. *That's* why I thought I could infiltrate fastest. Other than Izzy, no one else at the ATF knew you or the organization better." He leaned forward, rested his forearms on the table, and clasped his hands. "What I quickly realized, however, between recon and working with you, was that yours isn't the same organization Isabella, and those before her, had investigated. And you're getting out of the explosives business. I have no interest in stopping or arresting you."

"That's not what you said yesterday morning."

"You weren't listening."

He clasped the glass, knuckles white. "I was handcuffed to the fucking bed."

"You're not now," Chris said, fighting to keep this conversation focused, fighting not to get sidetracked by the image that flashed behind his eyes—Hawes naked and writhing and seething mad. So mad then, and now, that he still wasn't listening. "I need you to hear me, Hawes. *My mission remains the same*."

Hawes stifled a noise and averted his gaze, dropping his hand from the glass.

Helena took up the conversation. "To find Isabella's killer."

"Yes," Chris answered. "And also less death, which means stopping whoever is trying to overthrow you and your brothers. Our interests are aligned. We track the explosives and determine who is behind their theft and the attempted coup, and we stop them."

"We," Hawes scoffed. A flicker of something softer, sadder, passed across his eyes, before a sheet of ice slammed down over it. "I don't trust you."

"Then trust me," Kane spoke up. "I've got all sides of this covered."

Brows scrunched, lips pressed together again, Hawes did not look convinced by Kane's assertion, but the chief pressed on, and Chris kept his trap shut. He was getting nowhere, maybe Kane could.

"I do not want a bloodbath on my streets," Brax said. "Be it a war within your organization, an explosives sale to the wrong party, or a war between you and the ATF. I've got too much at stake here." More than just his job, given the strain in his body and the plea in his voice. "I'm trying to protect all of us. Trust me to do that and to keep my promise. Ten years and I haven't wavered. I won't now."

Hawes kept his gaze locked on Kane—calculating, assessing—for an interminable five seconds, before it flickered to Chris, then to the flash drive. He drew the device toward himself and pocketed it. "We'll consider it." He stood, Helena and Avery rising beside him.

Chris stood as well. "Thank you."

Helena gave him a departing, "Mr. Hair," Avery another stony glare, and for his part, Hawes paused at the door and leveled him with fiery blue eyes and a "Mr. Perri" that was a few octaves closer to last night's version. Chris counted it a win.

SIX

Monday morning arrived with no follow-up messages. Chris's phone was obnoxiously silent again, no matter how many times he'd checked it. Nothing from Hawes, nothing from Kane, not even an intrusion alert to indicate Holt was poking around in his system. Granted, there was a better than average chance Holt had circumvented his enhanced firewalls, but Chris fully expected the hacker to leave him a middle finger start-up greeting to let him know exactly where he'd been. But his computer, like his phone, transmitted no messages this morning.

Standing outside the 16th Street BART station, he glanced once more at his phone. Still nothing. An answer on how they were going to play this would be helpful sooner rather than later, given his babysitter's imminent arrival. He shoved the phone back into his pocket, rearranged his saddlebag so the strap crossed his body, then entered the teeming mass of commuters descending the stairs to the trains.

Taking BART one stop over to UN Plaza and the Federal

Building was easier than finding parking for the Hog downtown. Also quicker this time of morning, even with the broken escalators that plagued the stations. On second thought, maybe he should have taken the bike. He could have wasted time finding a parking spot and delayed facing the terror that was Scotty Wheeler.

By all accounts, Wheeler was a good agent, but he was not a UC agent. Need a tome-sized file built out for a case? Wheeler was the guy. Need to find a needle in a haystack? Wheeler was the guy. Need to delicately infiltrate a tight-knit family of assassins? Wheeler was so not the guy. He was about as subtle as a bag of hammers when it came to conducting investigations. And hammers were the last thing Chris needed when he was already skating on thin ice.

Once on the train, Chris shoved around the files in his bag and dug out his book. He hoped the starter files he'd spent all day yesterday preparing—on Amelia Madigan and the organization's soldiers—would keep Wheeler busy. Let Scotty dig for that particular needle while Chris went about his work, in his own way, relatively unimpeded.

He read a few pages before the doors slid open at the next stop. He exited the train onto the platform and into the sea of people, the tide moving slowly toward the stairs, as the escalator was broken at this station too. Packed in as they were, Chris didn't realize the person directly behind him was an enemy until they pressed the muzzle of a gun against Chris's lower back.

"No sudden movements, Agent Perri," the woman said.

A man appeared on Chris's other side, a half step back like the woman, but close enough to prick Chris's right flank with a knife, behind his bag and just above the waist-band of his jeans. "Keep walking," the man said.

Chris did as told but slowed his pace, enough that his would-be captors were forced by the crowd to pull even with Chris, giving him a better look. He recognized them from the pictures on his home office walls. Tamela with the gun to his left and Devon with the knife on his right. Madigan soldiers. Was this Hawes's answer? Or were Tamela and Devon working against their boss?

"Did Hawes send you?"

No comment, not that Chris had expected a reply. Soldiers knew better. But they did falter at the base of the stairs as the crowd in front of them undulated backward in response to a commotion on the level above.

An opening.

Chris heaved his paperback at the ceiling, scattering the rafter pigeons and jostling the platform crowd around them. Avoiding a knife to his kidneys, Chris slung his bag around to cover his lower back, spun toward Tamela, and grabbed her pistol by the barrel. It was a risk. She could pull the trigger and kill him, setting off a mass panic down here, but he was no good to them dead. She wouldn't fire.

It was the right call. Chris wrenched the gun from her grip and let momentum carry his right elbow back into Devon's face. Chris counterbalanced with a kick to the left, planting a boot in Tamela's stomach. Not enough to take her down, but enough to get the crowd really scattering.

Several of the closest bystanders screamed—"Fight!" "Move!" "Gun!"—having spotted the weapon in Chris's hand and Devon's combat knife clattering to the cement floor.

Chris had no choice. "ATF! Clear the area!" he shouted,

sealing the deal on chaos. Better for the public to know law enforcement was on the scene and better to announce himself to any converging BART Police. He'd reach for his badge if he could, but Devon, behind him, was trying to strangle him with the strap of his bag. Chris wedged his free hand under the strap, curled his fingers around it, and shoved outward, extending his arm. Victim to momentum again, Devon rammed into his back. Chris reached back his other arm, curled it around Devon's neck, and bending forward, hauled Devon over his back. The soldier hit the ground hard enough to knock the wind out of him, mouth opening and closing as he struggled for breath.

Chris was having trouble catching a breath—or break— of his own. Back on her feet, Tamela was preparing to attack. She shook out her limbs and eyed the gun Chris had trained on Devon.

Escalating shouts from the crowd drew Tamela's gaze off Chris long enough for him to tuck the gun into his waistband. He couldn't risk using it down here, even if most of the commuters had heeded the warnings and cleared out. With Tamela still distracted, Chris shrugged off his bag, wound the strap around his fist, and cocked it for a throw. Full of files, there was enough heft in the bag for a good hit.

The maneuver proved unnecessary.

A flash of gray silk, starched white cotton, and ice-blue eyes streaked in front of Chris, kicking back down a resurging Devon and sending Tamela to the ground beside him, the crack of bones unmistakable. She tilted forward, trying to curl over her awkwardly hanging arm, but the wire around her neck hauled her back upright.

"Not yours?" Chris said to the man holding either end of the garrote.

"Not anymore." Hawes leaned down and spoke right next to Tamela's ear. "Tell me why I shouldn't kill you, traitor."

Tamela didn't struggle or appear surprised. On the contrary, she looked satisfied. Downright smug.

The pieces snapped together in Chris's head. "Madigan, stop! It's what they want."

Hawes tightened the wire. "They're vetted."

"Why are you here?" Chris asked, snatching up Devon's knife.

"Got a tip."

"Exactly." He pointed at the black-domed cameras all along the platform and at the foot of the stairs. "There are cameras everywhere."

Hawes's smile was wicked. And beautiful. "Not anymore."

Chris tamped down the near overwhelming desire to kiss that deadly, gorgeous smile right off his face. He'd come for him. No, fuck, someone had sent him. "They may have information we can use."

Shouts echoed on the level above.

"ATF!"

"Police!"

"Move, move, move!"

"Guessing they got a tip too," Chris said to Hawes. "This is a setup, Madigan. Don't play into it."

"I knew what it was the second I got the tip, but I wanted to know who the rest of the traitors were. Now I know two more." He backed off and waited for Chris to secure Devon and Tamela. "And I had to be sure you—"

Inconveniently, the urge to kiss him crested again. "I can take care of myself too," Chris said instead. Not that he wouldn't have done the same thing, had he gotten a tip that Hawes was in mortal danger. Which was the very definition of going rogue, and Chris, recognizing that fact, still wouldn't do anything differently. He'd still race to save Hawes, for reasons beyond his value to the mission. Reasons that Chris needed to sort out, but not with the cavalry bearing down on them.

He shoved the gun and knife into his bag, not wanting either to trace back to the organization. From his experience with Amelia, he knew the soldiers wouldn't talk. The weapons were the only evidence. He thrust the bag at Hawes. "But thank you for the assist. Now get the fuck out of here."

He expected Hawes to take the bag and run. He did not expect Hawes to step closer, to shove a hand in his hair and wind it around his fist, to yank back Chris's head. "I still don't trust you." He crushed his mouth down onto Chris's, acting on the same adrenaline-fueled desire that had been riding Chris. A slide of lips, a swipe of tongue, a nip of teeth, a groan from each of them. The kiss was brief, stunning, breathtaking in its force and surprise, and Chris would have happily stayed right there in Hawes's arms if not for the official-sounding shouts a level above getting louder, closer.

Chris drew back and whispered, "Go," against Hawes's lips, then the king was gone, bag in hand, disappearing into the morning fog snaking through the train tunnels.

SEVEN

A fuming Scotty Wheeler was waiting for Chris in the field office lobby. "You let him get away."

"Let who get away?" Chris said, then flashed a smile at the receptionist, who tossed his access badge onto the counter. While the ATF's local division office was in Dublin, the smaller SF Metro office was Chris's home base when he was between assignments. Which was seldom enough that he didn't bother to keep—and lose—his access badge. Better to leave it here and claim it when needed.

Unneeded: Wheeler's welcome party. "Don't fucking play dumb with me, Perri." Wheeler turned on his heel and marched across the bullpen, the end of his tie flying over his suited shoulder. Always the properly dressed agent. Professional attire, clean-shaven, not a blond hair out of place. A far cry from Chris's beard, jeans, and tees, though he'd upgraded to a Henley today, owing to the office visit. He didn't even own a suit anymore. He'd tossed his only one the day after Izzy's funeral. The same day he'd tossed his hair clippers.

Wheeler spun in the conference room doorway, blocking Chris's entrance. He was shorter than Chris by a good half foot but packed into that compact body were muscles that spoke of daily hours spent in the gym. Not someone you wanted to tangle with. "Witness statements indicate a man matching Hawes Madigan's description was at the scene."

"But you've got no positive identification?"

"Don't I?" Wheeler stared up at him with big brown eyes that, on any other man, Chris would have considered attractive. Not, however, on the man who was about to make his life a living hell.

"Hawes Madigan was not at the scene." A phantom tingle ghosted over Chris's lips, reminding him that Hawes had most definitely been there.

Wheeler's ears and cheeks reddened with anger, the same frustration glittering in his dark eyes. He wanted to argue, but after a beat and a huffed breath, he thought better of it and retreated into the conference room. Chris bit back a victorious smile. Had he let it loose, it would have been short-lived, dying as soon as he entered the room and glimpsed Wheeler's work to date. File folders were scattered the length of the conference table, a flip board near the door was covered with pictures from both crime scenes last week, and the two wall-mounted whiteboards at the far end of the room were full of scribbled notes, including a Madigan org chart similar to the one Chris had constructed in his home office. Wheeler's chart had each party's official and unofficial capacity listed beneath their name, and off to the side, under the heading *Wildcard*, was written *Braxton Kane*.

Fuck.

Tran had lied. Wheeler hadn't just been put on this case.

This level of detail required weeks, months, years of work. Had Tran been running parallel investigations? And from the setup here, when had Wheeler actually arrived in town? Definitely before this weekend.

"You took those two operatives down by yourself?" Wheeler asked.

"I did."

"We'll see what they say when we question them."

Devon and Tamela had received medical attention at the scene and were now in the FBI's holding cells downstairs, neither cognizant enough yet for admissible interrogation. The SAC would let Chris and Wheeler know when they were ready. Not that Chris expected the soldiers to say much. If this went the way questioning Lucas and Amelia had, they'd stay mum. The opposing faction wanted to bring Hawes down and wrest control of the organization, not destroy it completely.

Chris strolled to the coffee maker at the other end of the room, checked it for water and fresh-enough grounds, then set it to brew. He rotated and rested back against the counter, gaze drifting again to Wheeler's case notes. "There's a flaw in your workup."

Wheeler turned halfway around to the board. "What's that?"

"The explosion after Cal's funeral was an attack on the Madigans, not one engineered by them."

"Amelia Madigan was behind it."

"Yes, but—"

"Let's get something straight, Perri." He shifted back around to face Chris. "Neither I nor the ATF care about whatever feud is going on in the Madigan organization. We're bringing it all down, starting at the top." He pointed at the picture of Hawes, sitting alone at the top of the pyramid. Another flaw in the workup, but Chris didn't clue Wheeler in on that one. If Wheeler wanted to focus his attention on Hawes, let him. Hawes could handle Scotty. There'd be less attention on Chris as he worked with Holt, Helena, and Kane on the thing that was supposed to matter to the ATF.

"According to Tran," Chris said, "the explosives are our primary objective."

"Which are where?"

Chris poured a mug of coffee and sipped in silence, not admitting to the unknown that was more dangerous than any of the Madigans.

"Exactly," Wheeler said, correctly reading his nonanswer. "You don't know where they are. Explosives made by professional assassins, which could land in the hands of even worse killers. I want to eliminate the organization that made them thereby stopping them from making more and eliminating those who could put the explosives to use."

That was one way to look at the situation. A bit Rambo-esque in its idealism, because fuck knew they couldn't eliminate all the targets.

"And you're going to help me," Wheeler added.

"What do you think I've been doing here? The past week with the Madigans, the past month of getting everything into place, the past three years following Izzy's leads? I'm trying to find a way in so we can identify the real killers and find the explosives."

"Well, you failed, King Slayer."

Chris gritted his teeth.

"Isn't that what they call you?"

There was a reason he understood Hawes's loathing of

his Prince of Killers moniker. A reason Chris knew exactly when to needle him with it and when to let it go. Because after taking down more than a few heads of criminal empires, Chris had earned his own moniker. One he liked about as much as Hawes liked his. Unfortunately, every time he slayed a king, collateral damage was unavoidable. Innocents wrapped up in the organization. Partners, kids, organization members who were just trying to do right by their families. Another reason why Hawes's new order had resonated with Chris, why he wanted to help him, not slay him. But Chris couldn't tell Wheeler any of that. "Yes, that's what they call me," he said instead.

Wheeler grinned, victorious. "Then let's slay the fucking king already."

If Chris had thought all eyes were on him Friday at SFPD headquarters, it was nothing compared to Monday afternoon. Badge around his neck, backup weapon holstered on his hip, he was no longer hiding his identity, and the curious looks were coming from all directions. He'd have to address the rumor mill at tomorrow's interagency task force meeting, but first he had a meeting with Kane—without Wheeler.

Maybe also with a certain Madigan.

Chris had mentally replayed that morning's altercation in the BART station too many times, like the best broken record ever. Hawes's too brief kiss, a phantom tingle on his lips that had lingered delightfully, torturously. His speed and skill in taking down Devon, the same agility and grace he'd displayed in dispatching Jodie. That wicked smile after. Chris couldn't get the scene—or the man—out of his head.

Trained in combat as he was, Chris found something undeniably sexy about a person whose skills rivaled his own, a person who exercised that much confidence and control over their faculties and surroundings. Even sexier had been Hawes ceding all that confidence and control to Chris in their moments alone last week. He'd done so because he'd trusted Chris, and Chris had betrayed that trust, though not to the extent Hawes believed. Chris had a way to go toward winning back that trust, but last night's meet and this morning's kiss were good starts. Granted, the brief lip-lock was ninety-nine percent fueled by adrenaline, but Chris could work with the one percent.

"You gonna stand out there all day?"

Kane's voice startled Chris back to the present. The chief was leaning his head and shoulders out his office door as if hiding something—*someone*—inside.

Chris's hope bloomed cautiously. "Sorry," he said. "Was going over some details from this morning in my head."

"We've got some other details to discuss." Kane inched the door open far enough for Chris to slip inside, then closed it behind him.

One look across the room and Chris's hope died, nipped in the bud by a wisp of disappointment and then a flood of concern. A folding table had been positioned in front of the shuttered bullpen window and the visitor chairs moved behind it. In one sat Jax, typing away on their laptop, and in the other sat Holt, with Lily strapped to his chest in a polka-dot sling.

He looked like utter hell.

The last time Chris had seen Hawes's fraternal twin was

Thursday, before Papa Cal's funeral. Holt had looked rough then. Four days and a mountain of shit later, the former soldier looked four-months-in-the-desert rough. Auburn beard untrimmed, freckled skin blotchy, brown eyes blood-shot and underlined by dark bags. Even his tattoo sleeve, peeking out from under the rolled right cuff of his flannel shirt, appeared dull. But as tired as he looked, his typing was no less sonic, the one-handed speed mind-boggling. He cradled Lily with his other arm, as if he were afraid to let his daughter go. She was out like a light, stealing the hours of sleep her father had clearly missed out on.

Kane collapsed into his protesting desk chair, which had been rolled to the short end of the folding table, closest to Holt. "He came in to meet with Amelia and her attorney."

Chris leaned a hip against Kane's desk and snagged a candy. "How'd that go?"

Holt lifted his fingers off the keyboard, then lifted his eyes, glaring daggers at Chris. "How do you think it went?"

Chris diverted to a safer topic. "How's Lily?"

"Misses her mom."

Or not so safe. The big man's tension only eased when Kane reached out and brushed his fingers over Lily's head.

Jax watched the quiet, familial moment fondly, unsur-prised. In fact, the IT specialist didn't appear surprised about any of what was going on here. "You're helping out on this case?" Chris asked them.

They jutted an orange nail at Holt. "I'm one of his kids."

Chris raised a brow. "One of his—"

"Jax was Holt's star mentee at the LGBTQ shelter," Kane supplied.

"Got my GED, then my BS, and started here last year."

How convenient. Another member of Team Madigan

here at the SFPD. A hacker. Any other time, Chris would worry about conflicts of interest, but more allies—and less traitors—were a good thing right now.

Kane reached behind Holt and picked up something off the floor. "I believe this is yours." He heaved Chris's saddlebag onto the table.

"You go through what was inside?"

"Of course," Holt answered. "Most of it was on the flash drive you gave us, though some of the additional…case-work…was…" Holt swallowed hard and averted his gaze —to Kane, to Lily, to his laptop. All the new materials had been about Amelia. More shit for Holt to bear while processing a broken heart. No wonder he looked like shit.

"Busy work for Wheeler," Chris said as he rifled through the folders and gave Holt time to gather himself. Everything except the weapons was still in the bag, including a new copy of the book he'd sacrificed to the pigeons. Ducking his chin, Chris hid his grin and lowered the bag to the floor. "Scotty's gonna be a problem," he said. "He's not just after the prototypes." Chris used the Madigans' code for the explosives, unsure how deeply Jax had been read in. "He's out to take your family down."

Holt's narrowed eyes darted up. "Scott Wheeler?" His fingers flew across the keyboard, and then he rotated the laptop toward Chris. "This guy?"

On-screen was Wheeler's profile page from the ATF's supposedly unhackable intranet. "That's him."

Holt cursed and snapped the laptop lid shut. "He was one of the feds posing as attorneys for the last buyer."

"At the meet last Tuesday?" Chris recalled Hawes's haste that morning. He'd turned down an offer of shower fun because he couldn't be late to that meeting. "For the sale of the prototypes?"

Holt nodded. "Hawes and I ran every feature we could remember through recognition databases until we got an ID. We weren't one hundred percent sure, but—"

"That's him, for sure. He's a good agent, but very by the book." Chris turned to Kane. "He's clearly been on this case longer than Tran led us to believe."

Kane rose, snagged a candy, and unwrapped it as he paced the threadbare carpet behind his desk. "She also led us to believe she'd call off the investigation if we secured the weapons. That's the ATF's jurisdiction."

Chris had thought so too, but he wasn't sure now. "Except jurisdiction gets murkier depending on who we find the prototypes with, how they came to be there, and if they can be traced back to the manufacturer."

"We're in the clear," Holt said. "They won't trace back to us."

"Someone could testify against you or manufacture evidence."

"Sure." Holt shrugged. "And I can manufacture evidence otherwise."

Kane tossed the balled-up candy wrapper at Holt and covered his ears with both hands. "Christ, Private."

One corner of Holt's mouth quirked up. Just the teensiest bit. Chris would have to buy Kane more candies.

"Any luck finding Amelia's missing flash drive?"

"So you admit you don't know where it is?" Holt countered.

Chris tilted his head. "In the new spirit of honesty."

Holt chuffed. Another good sign. "Fuck your honesty, but no."

Jax didn't hide their amusement, chuckling out loud before getting back to business. "What I do have is a new lead on the explosives." Read all the way in, then. They held out a tablet to Chris. Paperless—definitely one of Holt's kids. "This was posted on the dark web."

Chris took the tablet and read the solicitation on-screen. It was for bidders for a private auction of demolition proto-types happening tomorrow evening. The location would be provided to "pre-qualified bidders."

"You think this is your stockpile of explosives?"

"Pretty sure," Holt said. "We know from our last buyer that there was no one else in the market offering this much firepower."

"But why?" Chris asked. "If Amelia and her faction are after power, why are they selling off their most powerful weapons?"

"It's just a portion," Holt said.

"Funding the operation?" Kane ventured.

"Could be," Chris said. "Or it could be another trap like the one they tried to spring on Hawes this morning." He shifted his attention to Kane. "We'll have to prep the bust with multiple scenarios in play."

"We want to be there," Holt interjected.

"Did you fucking miss what I just said?"

"*We* have as much interest as *you* in finding out who's behind this."

Chris's frustration—and volume—rose to match. "Ask your fucking wife. She's not talking to any of the rest of us."

"You think I haven't tried!"

Lily's wail ended the argument as quickly as it had esca-lated. Chris backed off while Holt fussed over his agitated daughter.

"Madigans get eyes on," Kane offered as a compromise, his hand lightly clasping Holt's shoulder. "Jax, can you set up a closed channel?" They nodded, and then Kane said to Chris, "I'll give my team the order to capture, not kill. Will your team agree to the same?"

"I'll make it happen."

"I don't know if I can," Holt said to Kane. "I have to talk to—"

"Clear it with them." Kane squeezed his shoulder. "We'll get answers, but let us lock down the explosives first. It'll buy us all some breathing room."

"I'll see what I can do," Holt said with a nod.

Forward momentum. Chris wanted to cheer. At the same time, he worried his window for getting answers on Isabella's death was closing. Tran and Wheeler didn't care —their top priorities were the explosives and the Madigans, order debatable. While the night of Isabella's death marked a turning point for the Madigan organization, Hawes and his siblings' top priority now was holding on to control so they could keep the family and organization on the path they'd chosen. Chris was the only one putting Isabella first, and he couldn't let her down.

EIGHT

"Start with Devon," Chris told Wheeler, splitting his attention between his babysitter and the retreating backside of the FBI Special Agent in Charge who'd showed him to the interrogation rooms. Chris had heard stories—Irish accent, tailored three-piece suits, shiny cuff links, and a great ass—all true, except the SAC's rumored blond hair was in reality a far more attractive shade of red.

"He's been awake longer. He'll be more alert," Wheeler countered as he gathered his files off the table in the observation room. "We might get more out of the woman."

"We won't." If Chris had learned anything about Hawes's organization, it was that the women were the toughest. Given a choice between the three siblings at the top, Helena was the one he least wanted to meet in a dark alley.

Chris tucked his two file folders under his arm and stepped fully into the observation room, viewing Devon through the one-way glass. Cuffed to the table, the ex-

Madigan soldier was in better shape than his partner. Chris had broken Tamela's fingers when he'd snatched her gun away, and Hawes had broken her forearm when he'd interceded. Each of them had left shoe-size bruises on her torso, not to mention the "interesting" bruising around her neck. Chris had slipped the medic a Benjamin to sell that bullshit vagueness to Wheeler. By contrast, Devon had a few scrapes and bruises. He probably also ached from Chris's flip and Hawes's kick, but Devon hid those tells, sitting at attention in his chair.

"We don't have them on anything but assault," Chris said.

"You were a federal officer doing your job. Class D felony."

Chris leaned a shoulder against the wall next to the glass. "I was on my way to work. Not in the middle of an active operation."

"You sure they didn't have any weapons? Some of the witnesses—"

"Are mistaken. They were panicked by the altercation." He held one of his folders out to Wheeler. "Even if Devon did have a gun, he's got a permit for it, and it's clean. No criminal history on it."

Wheeler flipped through the papers, then snapped the file shut. His gaze flickered to the mirror and back. "He doesn't know that."

Chris bet Devon did, but Wheeler was done arguing. He shoved the folder against Chris's chest, grabbed his own off the table, then stepped past him. He held the interrogation room door open for Chris, and the two of them entered, claiming the chairs across the table from Devon.

"Mr. Henderson," Wheeler said.

"Devon," the soldier corrected.

Wheeler pushed a piece of paper across the table. "This is your signed Miranda waiver. You can change—"

"Unnecessary," Devon said. "No attorney needed." He was as calm and confidently resigned as Lucas had been on Hawes's yacht. This was fucking useless.

"You work for Madigan Cold Storage?" Wheeler said.

"Worked. Recently quit."

As in this morning. Chris stifled his scoff.

Wheeler thankfully didn't notice. "Why was that?"

"Didn't like the direction the company was headed."

"What direction was that?"

Devon's gaze drifted to Chris, even as he answered Wheeler. "Management got more selective of their clientele. Didn't seem like the best business decision for growing the company."

"What exactly did you do for Madigan Cold Storage?" Wheeler's restraint impressed Chris. He was drilling down on Devon's cover instead of going straight for reality.

"Marketing," Devon answered.

"Why does a marketing professional need a forty-five and a concealed carry permit?"

"Personal reasons."

"Like the fact that you're an assassin for the Madigans."

"I closed deals for my former employer." No widening eyes, no twitching lips, no reaction whatsoever.

Chris didn't expect any less. He did, however, expect Wheeler to follow the line of questioning about the history of the gun.

The other agent swerved instead. "Why did you attack Agent Perri at the BART station this morning?"

"My associate and I only wanted to have a conversation

with him. He"—Devon tilted his head toward Chris—"escalated the situation."

Bullshit, but Chris couldn't say that without disclosing the weapons he'd denied the presence of to Wheeler. Avoiding that possible question, Chris asked a different one. "What did you want to discuss with me?"

"The weather."

No holding in that scoff.

"Who took you down?" Wheeler asked. "At the station."

"Agent Perri."

"Alone?"

"Not my finest moment."

Wheeler did not let up. "Was Hawes Madigan at the scene?"

"I don't know where Mr. Madigan was this morning. I'm no longer his employee."

Wheeler was missing the point, lost in details that didn't matter. Chris focused on the forest instead. "Whose employee are you, Devon?" He leaned forward, resting his forearms on the table. "You're someone's. I know that much, and it's not Hawes Madigan's. Nor is your boss Amelia Madigan. She hasn't spoken to anyone but her counsel since her arrest."

The assassin clammed up. Not so chatty anymore.

"What was the plan?" Chris pressed. "Kill me? Lure Hawes to the rescue so you could frame him?" Chris chose his next words carefully. "Clear the way for your boss to take over the company?"

More silence.

Chris opened his other file folder, took out the single

sheet of paper inside it, and slid it across the table. He'd wheedled the printout from Kane, over Holt's strenuous objections, and only after Jax had assured their mentor they'd isolated the printer and data from SFPD's network. "Is your boss the one engineering this auction?"

Devon's eyes widened a fraction, and his breath stuttered once. An average observer wouldn't notice the reaction, but Chris caught it. The flash of surprise that law enforcement was onto them. Seeing it too, Wheeler leaned forward to peer at the paper. Chris held his breath until Wheeler sat back in his chair, trap still thankfully shut.

Chris continued with his line of questioning. "Why?" he asked, trusting Devon would understand the question.

"Same answer, Agent Perri. I don't agree with the current direction of the company. If MCS wants to stay at the top of the market, maybe it's time for some new blood."

Threats and judgments wrapped in slick marketing lingo. Devon played his cover well, except for the clue he'd dropped.

Chris reached for the printout and tucked it back into its folder. "I'm good here." He stood. "Thank you, Mr. Henderson. We'll be keeping you in custody until we have a chance to question your associate."

Devon smiled. "I'll take that lawyer now."

Chris bet he would. Now the traitor was in a hurry, no doubt eager to avoid a night in jail and to relay to his boss that law enforcement was onto their plan.

"We'll get right on that," Chris lied.

Wheeler followed him back into the observation room. "What was that printout about? An auction?"

Chris shoved the folder at him. "Read up. And make

sure no one gets in there with him. I don't want word to get back to his boss, whoever that is, that we know about this."

"We should question—"

"She'll tell you less, trust me."

Wheeler backed down, the second time in the last few minutes. Good. They needed to be on the same page in their approach to this case. And Chris could use Wheeler's help. He needed the agent who could find the needle. "Briefing's in an hour. We've got work to do."

Night had fallen and the fog had rolled back in by the time Chris emerged from the BART station and walked the several blocks west toward Mission Dolores. The city park and mix of residential and commercial buildings gave his neighborhood a bustling vibe, no matter the hour, but the cool summer night had driven some folks inside, the foot traffic on his street lighter than usual.

The person sitting halfway up his porch steps, however, didn't seem the least bit fazed by the cold. Bundled in a puffy teal vest, his niece sat with a pink pastry box on her knees and an e-reader in her hands, index finger swiping pages. Her nose was rarely out of a book, electronic or otherwise. She'd come by that honestly.

Chris rounded the front of the cement stairs and propped a boot on the bottom step. Mia glanced up but only for a second before she went back to reading. "Got those mistletoe cannoli for you."

"You've also got keys to the place. Why didn't you let yourself in?"

She shrugged one shoulder. "After that heatwave last week, I'm savoring the cold."

"It was one day." Tuesday. When Hawes's grandfather had died. There'd been a few hours of sun on Friday too, but it had disappeared as quickly as it had come, just like his cover had gone poof that day.

"One too many," Mia said, bringing him back to this week. She tucked her e-reader into her vest pocket and stood. "I had to take my breaks in the pastry freezer."

Chuckling, Chris climbed the rest of the way up the stairs and opened the front door. His niece breezed inside, flipping on lights as she strolled down the hallway toward the kitchen, more at home here than he was. When she'd turned thirteen, he'd started paying her twenty bucks a month to check on the place when he was gone. Other than annually upping her rate, she'd never once complained, happy to have her own private sanctuary. He blocked out the thoughts of what else his teenage niece might have used his place for. And the worry that she resented him for returning and taking away her refuge. He'd like to avoid a pissed-off teenager; they were scary, or at least he had been when he was a teen, before things had changed.

Mia dropped the pastry box on the island. "So, who you bribing with these?"

"A tech at SFPD. They did me a favor." He peeked under the lid, mouth watering. "Thanks for bringing them over. You didn't have to. I was gonna pick them up this weekend."

"Was in the neighborhood."

Chris lifted a brow. Mission Dolores wasn't completely on the other side of town from North Beach, but it also wasn't on Mia's way home from AB's, where she was working for the summer.

"Ethan lives a couple blocks over," she added.

"The boyfriend?"

She cocked a hip and put both hands on her waist. At the same time, her face took on a wistful expression. "He's more than just a boyfriend."

Ah, young love. Chris would rather deal with the pissed-off-teenager version of his niece. "You being safe?" That ought to do it.

Sure enough, Mia's dreamy expression vanished with an annoyed eye roll and dramatic, put-upon sigh.

Chris laughed. No sense getting angry back; that wouldn't get him the answer he needed. He circled the island, opened the fridge, and pulled out two pints of Blue Bottle NOLA iced coffee. He bumped the door shut with his elbow and set the cartons on the island.

"Ooh…" Mia's dark eyes lit up. "One of those for me?"

Chris kept a hand on both. "When you answer the question."

Another eye roll, but this time accompanied by a huff of laughter. "Yes, Davos, we're being safe."

He scoffed, over-the-top and gasping for effect. "I'm not that old!" He slid a carton across the counter, then held up both his hands, wiggling his fingers. "And I have all of these."

Mia cut her eyes to the pastry box as she worked open the coffee. "And yet you're smuggling out-of-season cannoli as bribes."

"Touché. In that case…" He flipped open the box lid and snagged a cannoli, setting it on a paper towel he'd ripped from the roll. "Smuggler's tax."

Before he could take a bite, Mia shoved a hand under his nose, palm up. "Call me Salladhor, then."

Chris couldn't help but smile. She was whip-smart, having outpaced him in reading their favorite series, and witty, having outpaced him in this conversation. Sassy, just like her mother...used to be.

He handed her one of the white chocolate, pistachio, and cranberry confections, a cannoli version of the white chocolate-dipped pistachio and cranberry biscotti Grandma Perri used to make for Christmas. At first bite, they both hummed in delight, then enjoyed a few minutes of companionable silence as they ate.

But Chris hadn't forgotten where his thoughts had left off. "How's your mom?"

"Fine." Too fast, too short. And too obvious in her effort to look anywhere but at him. She polished off her coffee and wandered over to the dining table, shuffling through the books there. She stopped when her hand landed on the hardback at the bottom of the stack, fingers tracing the faded gold seal on the cover. "This was her favorite. She used to read it to me whenever I came over here to play. Mom wouldn't let me have it."

"You remember that? You were only five."

She smiled fondly, genuinely, a rare sight on her fifteen-year-old face, and lowered herself into the closest chair. "Of course I remember. She was my best friend. I worshipped her."

Chris tossed their empty cartons, then claimed the seat next to her. "She used to read it to me too, every night before bed. I lost count how many times we went through it. She'd read, I'd make the character noises. It never seemed to scare her."

"Scared the shit out of me, but it was worth it. Because she loved it so much." Mia turned glassy eyes toward him, her tears held hostage by sheer will. Not so much in her voice, though, as she croaked out, "I miss her."

Chris threw an arm around his niece and hugged her close. "So do I. Every day." He swallowed hard, fighting back his own tears. This was the hardest part of being back here. What he'd avoided for the past ten years. Picking up the pieces of a life lost and trying to put it back together. Unlike Hawes and the Madigans, he'd taken the easy route and run from his pain, from his demons, when he should have held close the family he had left. How much damage had he done—to all of them —by leaving things a scattered mess? Was it too late to fix this? Could he really come home again, like his mom had said?

And what of Hawes? Was he part of the picture of home? Did he belong in the puzzle? And if he did, where did he fit when both of them kept bending the edges and changing the shape of the piece?

As if reading the direction of his thoughts, Mia asked through her sniffles, "Are you back? Nonna said…"

"I'm thinking about it."

That got her attention. She drew back and looked up at him with a raised brow. "For real?" she asked, a bit of fire back in her voice.

"For real." He reached behind him for the roll of paper towels, tore one off, and handed it to her. "But I didn't want to get your hopes up until I was more sure."

She blew her nose, graceless and uninhibited, and Chris's heart swelled, loving her all the more for it. But then his heart broke at her next words. "We need some hope,

Uncle Chris." She sounded like her mother, far too weary, more so than any fifteen-year-old kid should ever be.

The investigator reared his head, but he gentled his voice. This was his family. He needed to be Uncle Chris here, not Agent Perri. "You want to tell me what's going on?"

"Adults don't think kids notice." She punched her nails through the paper towel, ripping it apart. "They think we don't know what's going on."

But certain lessons from his professional life were applicable here. "You know," he said, "if I'm at a crime scene and there's a kid among the bystanders, or God forbid directly involved, they're the first person I go to. They see more than anyone." He reached out and closed a hand over Mia's. "Tell me what you see, Mia."

"Mom's so unhappy, and Dad…"

She stiffened, a slight shiver she covered with a shake of her dark hair, and both the investigator and the uncle saw red. Only his ten years of undercover work kept Chris calm —because that's what Mia needed—but his anger was barely contained. "Has he hurt you?"

She shook her head again. "No, but I worry about Mom and about Marco. The example he's setting. It's toxic."

"Marco's a good kid."

"He's twelve and impressionable. Just last week he decided yellow was his favorite color because the cute camp counselor likes yellow. In the spring it was purple because that was the favorite color of the kid he liked in class." The ramble and accompanying eye roll were enough to temper Chris's fury. "You'd make a better impression," she said. "We need you." Her plea shifted him fully back into uncle mode.

He circled her shoulders again and squeezed. "I'm always here for you, Mia."

"Here"—she jostled against his side—"and on the phone aren't the same thing."

No, they weren't. They were further apart than Chris had realized. And the urgency to close that distance ratcheted up another notch on his priority ladder.

NINE

Chris hadn't expected the explosives to be at the auction. Strategically and tactically, it made no sense. Too big a stockpile to transport and too big a risk to take until a deal was made. Close by, though, was a reasonable assumption. That had been his and Wheeler's assertion to the joint task force yesterday. So when word had come down an hour ago —Holt via Kane—that the auction would take place this evening in one of Potrero Hill's new mixed-use buildings, Chris had savored a small victory.

Potrero was in the target vicinity if the explosives were at one of the old Hunter's Point piers on the other side of Highway 101 or in a warehouse just down the peninsula in South City, near where the Madigans had originally stored them. Chris had already sent agents out to both areas, but nothing so far. He radioed for them to step up their searches. Better shot of victory there than at the auction site itself.

Right on the neighborhood's main drag, the building was six stories high with commercial space on the ground floor and residential units on the five floors above. None of the units had balconies, the windows were irregularly shaped and spaced, and all of the building's glass was that godforsaken green-tinted shit that was all over the city now.

A bitch to adequately surveil, compounded by the weekday rush hour. Impossible to evacuate or cordon off without alerting the auction organizer. Challenging to identify whether people entering the building were residents, customers, or targets. It was a tactical nightmare and cleverly chosen for precisely that reason.

And because the top floor units were vacant.

There'd been a delay obtaining the materials for the penthouses' luxury interior finishes. While most of the rest of the building was open and operating, the top floor wasn't ready for renters yet. Chris was sure the auction organizer knew that too.

"Got one!" Jax called, voice raised over the traffic in the room.

Chris turned from the window he'd been staring out. They were two buildings over from their target, and all they could initially see from here—their makeshift joint task force command in a vacant commercial space—was the sidewalk leading to the target building. Jax, however, had secured them a better view via the camera in the nonoperational sidewalk ATM. It was supposed to go live next week, when the lobby-level bank it was attached to officially opened. Two calls—one to the local FBI, then another to the local US attorney—and Chris had a court order for the bank to partially power on the ATM. To passersby, it looked dead —no lit screens, no cash to dispense—but Jax had accessed the machine's camera, giving them a view of who was coming and going.

"Who is it?" Wheeler said as he crossed from the far corner where he'd been standing with the tactical team.

One of the monitors on the table they'd set up as Jax's workstation flickered to life and displayed the face captured from the ATM.

"I'll take human trafficker for five hundred, Alex," Jax quipped. Another burst of keystrokes, and a picture of the cartel captain appeared on-screen, together with his mile-long rap sheet.

Glee flashed across Wheeler's face, swift and ruthless, before he remembered to conceal it. Composed once more, he peppered the tactical team with follow-up questions. A bigger opportunity had presented itself, and Wheeler would pluck all the tail feathers he could.

By contrast, Chris was desperately trying to staunch the wave of bile climbing his throat. Hawes would be devastated if his family's explosives fell into the cartel's hands. He was taking the organization in the opposite direction. Hell, he'd been systematically cutting down the cartel over the past few months, not aiding them.

Chris remembered his wall art at home—the "outsider" he'd marked with an X on the right side of the org chart. Was the cartel the outsider player here? Were they trying to remove the threat against them by engineering a coup against Hawes? It made tactical and logical sense, but Chris had a hard time believing Amelia would ally herself with an organization that traded in drugs and flesh. She had her faults, had fallen prey to the temptation of power, but everyone had a redline, and Chris didn't think she'd cross this one.

"Got another!" called Lance, the ATF agent running the station next to Jax.

Behind them, Wheeler paled and moved a hand toward his sidearm as if on instinct. A face flashed up on the screen next to Lance, and Chris almost lost his battle against the bile. He understood Wheeler's reaction, understood why every LEO in the room had gone on high alert. Chris didn't need to see the rap sheet. They all knew this asshole. A white supremacist with a rabid online following, who was connected to half a dozen domestic terrorism incidents, who always managed to slip free of charges, and who was suspected of making threats against immigration offices in sanctuary cities, including San Francisco. And here he was in Chris's city, bidding on weapons to do just that. Again. Same as he'd tried to do the night Izzy had died. It had been the last report she'd logged before her murder. Was this—*today*—connected to that night three years ago? Was this more than just an attempted coup?

Chris's stomach roiled, forcing him to turn away and catch his breath. Splaying a hand on the window, he waited for the cool glass to temper his boiling insides. Slow going, but better than punching a hole through the wall, or worse, outwardly railing while Wheeler was on the horn with Homeland Security.

"This isn't what they wanted," Kane said, joining him at the window.

"I know." If the explosives landing with the cartel captain would devastate Hawes, that much firepower falling into the hands of a dangerous bigot—one who'd use it against their city—would be more than Hawes's soul could handle. "He's just trying to protect them," Chris said as he looked down at the packed sidewalk. "All these people going about their rush-hour business. Oblivious to the threat walking among them. Unaware that if those explosives fall into the wrong hands, they could be dead tomorrow."

"All this just to fund the takeover."

Chris glanced over at Kane. "That what this feels like to you?"

The chief didn't reply.

"Me neither," Chris said. "Something's off."

"Target Alpha sighted," Lance said, and Chris whirled around, not believing his fucking ears.

No denying his eyes, though. The screen grab from the ATM didn't lie. Dark, fitted suit, dark dress shirt, blue eyes bright, and light-brown hair ruffling in the breeze. Hawes Madigan. Chin held high, beautiful sharp angles on display, he walked right into the last place on earth he was supposed to be. Imperious, confident, like he owned the place.

"Can you zoom out?" Chris said to Jax.

A few keystrokes later, they had a wider view of Hawes and his surroundings. And of the absence of other operatives. He was alone.

"Fuck!" Chris cursed.

Jax shot him a worried look, while Wheeler shouted new orders to the tactical teams. "Madigan is on-site. Move him to priority one!"

"The explosives are priority one!" Chris insisted. "The stockpile and the seller are our primary targets."

"And I'm not convinced Hawes Madigan isn't our seller," Wheeler countered. "If it turns out you're right and he's not, then so be it. But he's still an agency target. I can get him, the weapons, the seller, plus two other criminals."

That same glee streaked across his face again, too overpowering to contain. "It's going to be a good day."

Or one of the worst days of Chris's life.

"Heat signatures indicate bidders are going to separate units on the top floor. Three total." Jax didn't have to raise their voice now that only a handful of people remained. The tactical teams, comprised of ATF agents and SFPD officers, had left command thirty minutes ago, moving into position at or near the auction site. Dressed in plain clothes over fitted tactical gear, they entered the building as if they were residents or shoppers. They'd hold there until Wheeler ordered them to the next position.

"Any indication of who and where the seller is?" Wheeler asked.

"Don't know who," Jax said, "but maybe this room here." The building was U-shaped, and the penthouse Jax indicated was at the top end of the southeast wing, as far as possible from the other occupied units, which were on the west and north sides of the building.

"The bend to the southeast wing would be guarded against anyone who started up the hall to the isolated unit," Chris said.

Jax nodded. "And just across the hall is a service elevator. Separate access versus the common area elevator the buyers traveled up." They pointed to the main bank of elevators at the center of the building, the bottom of the U.

"Anything else?" Kane asked.

"Two other people headed up the north stairwell, but they turned back and exited on five."

"Probably just residents that were talking and went too far," Wheeler said. "What about on the top floor? Any other movement?"

"Someone is going back and forth from the isolated room to the other units."

"Ferrying bids," Chris surmised.

Wheeler gestured to the heat signature of the person who remained in the presumed seller's room while the runner went back and forth between it and the others. "That still figure must be Madigan."

Here we go again.

"Not him," Chris said. "He's not the seller."

"If he's not the seller, then what the fuck is he doing there?"

Chris jabbed a finger toward the seller's room. "Trying to figure out who that is, just like us." Then he gestured at the other rooms. "And trying to figure out if any of them are in on it. He doesn't do business with people like these anymore."

"Or he's the third buyer," Wheeler said, pointing at the three buyer-occupied rooms. "There to buy back the explosives. I've got him, Perri, one way or the other."

"For fuck's sake, Scotty, he's trying to keep them away from the others."

Kane stepped between them, voice calm and level. "The explosives aren't here. We've gone over this."

"But someone in that building *will* take us to the explosives." Wheeler turned away and raised the comm to his mouth. "Teams, move into second positions."

Chris cursed again and retreated to the opposite corner. "What the hell are they doing?" he asked when Kane joined him. "This is not *eyes only*."

Kane held his phone so Chris could see the log of unanswered calls to Holt. "He's not answering me or Jax."

That niggle of doubt in the back of Chris's mind blew loud as an air horn. Louder still as Wheeler radioed the teams to converge on the fifth floor, one below the penthouses. "If this auction isn't about funding the coup, then what's it about?" Chris said.

"Power," Kane replied. "That's what it's always been about. Hawes and his siblings have it. The opposition wants it so they can take the organization in a different direction. Backward."

Chris picked up the thread. "So assume this auction is about power too. The seller arranged the buyers like that on purpose. Into separate rooms and only communicating through a runner."

"The seller is keeping each buyer on a string, controlling them," Kane said. "They can keep the auction going or shut it down."

Control. Shut it down.

The words, the niggle, resolved into a single sound, a single thought. This auction wasn't about alliances with outsiders or only wiping Hawes off the map. It was about consolidating power, period. "Fuck! It's a trap." As Chris had thought it might be, but not for the reason and person he thought. "Not just for Hawes."

"They want to take out the buyers," Kane followed.

Chris nodded. "And with all those agents and officers in there too. "Fuck!" Chris moved to go, but Kane grasped his forearm.

"You stay, I'll go."

"Brax."

Hard hazel eyes clashed with his. "I made a promise."

"To Hawes?"

"As good as." He shifted his gaze to Wheeler. "And you need to stay here to convince him to evac. He won't listen to me, but he might listen to you. You have to get him to pull back."

Kane didn't give Chris a chance to argue. He released his arm and sprinted toward the exit. Chris didn't waste time either, charging toward Wheeler. "Pull back! It's a trap!"

Jax spun in their chair. "What?"

"They're going to blow the place."

"Hawes?" Wheeler said. "The Madigans?"

"No!" Chris shouted. "The person who wants him dead." He gestured emphatically at the buyer-occupied rooms. Rooms with major underworld players waiting in them like sitting ducks. "And them too. Everyone who might challenge their power."

Wheeler hesitated. Good. "Do you know that for sure? The bust we could make—"

"Isn't worth our agents' or innocent lives."

"We don't know—"

"Agent Wheeler," Jax called. "Seller and runner are on the move."

He and Chris both whipped around. "Which direction?"

"Down the service elevator."

"They're leaving the scene," Chris said. "Before they put some of those explosives to use."

A radio crackled and a broken voice came through, resolving after a moment. "Beta team to command." Wheeler radioed back confirmation, and the team leader continued. "We've got a device in the north stairwell."

Wheeler's eyes grew wide. "What kind of device?"

"Receiver for a remote detonator."

"Can you disarm it?"

The service elevator opened on the bottom floor. They had seconds before the seller and runner left the building. And blew it. "There's no time," Chris said.

Wheeler didn't hesitate. "Abort! Pull the alarms, clear the lower floors. Emergency evacuation protocols." Wheeler shoved a radio into Chris's hand. "Help me coordinate."

Sirens rent the air, and residents—and LEOs—began pouring out of the building. All Chris wanted to do was run in there and make sure Hawes got out alive too, but Kane was already on it. Chris had to prioritize getting the residents, agents, and officers out.

"Jax," he said. "Keep an eye on that service exit. Tap and record nearby footage." Chris waited for their nod, then returned his attention to where it was needed. He raised the radio to his mouth and worked in tandem with Wheeler to expedite the evac.

Wheeler was doing a sit-rep with his teams when Jax interrupted. "Agent Perri, something you need to see." He expected footage around the service door, a possible ID on the seller. Instead, they pulled up the heat signatures on the top floor again and rewound the past two minutes. While agents and officers had been busy clearing the lower floors, and the seller and runner had been on their way down the service elevator, the buyers in their rooms had done…nothing. They were perfectly still.

Too still.

"What the fuck?" Chris was still trying to put it together when, behind them, Wheeler confirmed, "Lower floors are clear."

"What about Kane?" Jax asked. "Where's the chief?"

Wheeler radioed, to no response. Chris tried as well, to no better.

"Is he up on the top floor?" Wheeler asked. "What's going on there?"

"Buyers are still in their rooms," Jax answered vaguely with a flick of their eyes to Chris.

"Can we move on—"

Whatever Wheeler was going to say, the answer was no they couldn't. Windows shattered, a boom echoed, and one half of the top floor erupted into flames.

With Hawes and Kane still in there.

Chris's heart stopped, then fell to his feet along with his acid-filled stomach. He grabbed hold of Jax's chair, struggling to keep the rest of his weight from collapsing at the loss.

He didn't want to believe it. He closed his eyes, blocking out the smoke and fire and praying that this awful reality was like Izzy's voice in his head, a figment of his imagination. That any sign of an explosion would be gone when he opened them again. No such luck. In reality, the smoke billowed darker and the flames burned brighter.

Two good men. Gone. A friend and competent law-enforcement officer in Kane. Something infinitely more intriguing, more promising, in Hawes. The chance at something real together was slim—a lawman and a man constantly hunted by the law, that only happened in the books he read—but fuck if that slim possibility hadn't infiltrated his mind as deeply as he'd infiltrated Hawes's organization.

And now that puzzle piece was gone. Not just the corners bent and ragged from the past week of shifting truths. Gone, and in that second, Chris tossed out the question of whether Hawes had been a piece of that home puzzle for him. The picture of home—at least the one in Chris's head—would be incomplete without him. He'd be a third missing piece, like the one lost a decade ago and the Izzy-shaped one three years gone now.

And fuck, if the gaping emptiness in Chris's chest was enough to steal his breath, he hated to think how Helena and Holt would react when word reached them. After losing Papa Cal to death, then Amelia to prison, could the family come back from a double hit like this?

Chris's feet—his soul—itched with the need to run. Dive back into his case, into oblivion. But how, when his best leads on Izzy's killer were gone? Working with Hawes, with the Madigans, with Kane, had been his best shot at the truth. No one else would avenge his partner. Tran had made that clear. Chris had been closer than anyone else, closer than he'd ever managed from afar. And now all that was gone too.

Mission fail.

While Chris fought to keep himself upright, Wheeler paced on the other side of the table, raking a hand through his hair. Not so perfectly coiffed anymore. "Can you get any readings?"

"Fire's too hot on the top floor," Jax replied. "Checking the lower... Wait... I've got four bodies coming down the service stairwell."

"Alpha team, converge on the service stairwell exit," Wheeler ordered. "Possible targets—"

The service door, in sight of the ATM camera and over

half a dozen tactical helmet cams, banged open. Out of the billowing smoke walked two men, each with a child in his arms. Two men Chris had never been so happy to see in his life.

"Stand down!" he forced out around his hammering heart, which had rocketed from his feet up into his throat. "Stand down!"

Wheeler gasped. "That's Madigan."

"And Kane," Chris shot back. "Carrying two kids rescued from a burning building, so for once in your goddamn life, stand the fuck down!"

Quelled, Wheeler raised one hand and lifted the radio in his other, relaying the order to stand down. "I just want to talk to Madigan," he said, once temperatures in the room had cooled.

"So do I, but he's not going anywhere." Chris nodded at the surveillance feeds, which showed Hawes and Kane across the street from the building now, being mobbed by relieved parents and residents, while EMS and law-enforcement officers waited at the edge of the crowd. They were hemmed in. And if that weren't enough, at either end of the block were press vans. "You'll get your chance. But Hawes Madigan just saved two kids, and together with Kane, who knows how many other agents, officers, and residents."

Wheeler jabbed an accusing finger at the other monitor, at the top floor of the building that continued to blaze. "While he let the buyers burn."

TEN

As bad as it initially looked, the explosion had been relatively contained. Newly constructed, the building was equipped with all the latest fire-suppression equipment, and SFFD had been close by and on alert for operation support. Only the top-floor penthouses occupied by the buyers had been materially damaged.

Just enough to cover the evidence. Exactly as the clever auction organizer had intended. With a few hours' distance from the event now, Chris had worked out the math. Adding together the too still buyers he'd glimpsed on-screen just before the explosion, plus the charred remains of the bodies they'd found in the penthouses, plus what he'd learned of the way this new generation of Madigans viewed their role in dispensing justice, the sum of the equation was obvious.

It had been a fucking job. Either orchestrated by the Madigans, or neatly taken advantage of when the opportunity had presented itself. Regardless, Chris was fucking pissed. He'd been left out of the fucking loop, his and

Kane's people had been recklessly endangered, and worst of all, he'd had to watch Hawes walk into a trap, think him caught, and for two harrowing minutes, believe him dead. He'd made Chris doubt his mission, his purpose, his burgeoning plan to stay here and make a home. Made him forget about being the uncle Mia and Marco needed, the brother Celia could rely on, and the son Gloria deserved. Hawes had sent his insides on a roller coaster and almost made him run.

And for what? A goddamn power trip. A war that, while seemingly connected to Izzy's death, wasn't going to stop if Chris solved the latter. A battle Hawes and his siblings clearly intended to fight on their own. Granted, Chris being on the outside looking in was in no small part due to his own betrayal, but this was about more than just him. Holt had sat there in Kane's office, looked them in the eye, and given no indication that this was anything but the op they were planning. And that order had no doubt come from Hawes, who'd risked more than just his own life.

But Chris couldn't be angry with him, literally. The target of his rage had dodged him in the hours since the blast, all while being treated like a fucking hero. Local news channels ran a loop of the footage of Hawes and Kane emerging from the building with those kids, and even the agents and officers were handling Hawes with kid gloves.

Everyone except Wheeler, who didn't buy that Hawes just happened to be in the building this evening to view one of the penthouse units. Didn't buy that Hawes hadn't reached his destination before the explosion. The property's sales manager had vouched for Hawes, of course. Had that been the person who'd stayed in the "seller's room" while Hawes ran back and forth to the buyers? Chris wondered how much Hawes had paid the guy to risk his life and jail time.

Wheeler didn't believe Hawes or the property manager, but he'd let it go, temporarily. He'd been too busy cleaning up the almost mess he'd made sending agents into a hot zone. Kane had likewise been busy dealing with SFPD's role in the situation, while also fielding media requests and stifling his own boiling anger. Chris wasn't sure which of them was more irate. Kane had also been left out of the loop, inadvertently endangered his officers, and run into a wired-to-blow building to "save" a friend's life. Chris was sure Hawes and company would hear about it from the chief, if they survived Chris's wrath first. As angry as he was, he might earn that King Slayer title Wheeler was so damn eager to pin on him. The risks Hawes had taken today, if Chris was right, were too fucking high.

He was so mad, so distracted running scenarios in his head of what he'd do to Hawes Madigan if he could only fucking find him, that Chris almost fell on his ass when he walked into his condo and found his target standing next to the kitchen island, drinking a beer. Free of soot and suit, dressed in jeans and a Giants pullover, Hawes looked like he'd just returned from the ballpark, not like he'd barely escaped an explosion.

"Mr. Perri."

Standing in the foyer, Chris was battered by the emotional dissonance. Relief, surprise, desire, and the heated anger that had simmered all evening, rising to a rolling boil and burning away the other emotions. But he'd be damned if he let Hawes see that. Not until he got his fucking answers.

Chris shrugged off his coat and hung it on the rack by

the door. Small, everyday motions to keep the rage banked. Innocent, conversational questions to lead into the big ones. "You adding breaking and entering to your rap sheet?"

"Wouldn't be the first time."

Chris measured his steps down the hallway, forcing his gait to remain casual as he passed Hawes on the way to his bedroom. "You found where I lived," Chris said as he moved around the room. He opened his closet and secured his sidearm in the safe with the other empty holster.

Hawes rattled around in the kitchen. "Once I had the name right, it wasn't too hard."

Chris checked to make sure the locked door to the room between his bedroom and the study was secure and untampered with, then headed back out to deal with his intruder. "I'm sure it wasn't hard for Holt," he said, coming to stand beside Hawes at the kitchen island.

Hawes handed him an open bottle, then took a long drag from the fresh one he'd helped himself to. "He's good at what he does."

"Which I'm guessing isn't being a messenger."

"Oh, he's good at that too. 'Eyes only.' I heard you. I just didn't listen."

"Or you set it up to start with."

Hawes grinned around the mouth of his bottle, and it took every bit of restraint Chris had to wait until Hawes lowered the bottle from his lips before snatching it out of his hand and slamming it on the tiled countertop.

So much for playing it cool. At least he hadn't broken the bottle. "What the fuck were you thinking?"

Hawes, by contrast, was the epitome of cool. Of controlled. Hip to the island, he rotated to face Chris. "Why should I tell you anything? I don't trust you."

"Then why are you here?"

"You think I want to be?"

Chris scoffed. "Please, you wouldn't be here if you didn't want to be."

"I *shouldn't* be here." A flash of fire in those eyes, a crack in the ice of that cool exterior. "I don't trust you. But after today, you're the only one who—" He cut himself off and turned his face away, made to move away too, but Chris grabbed his wrist and held his hand to the bar.

A sharp inhale. More cracks.

Chris wanted the rest of that sentence. Wanted to swallow that inhale. Desperately, on both counts. But he still needed fucking answers. Needed to make clear that today couldn't happen again, for everyone's sakes.

"You left me and Kane out of the loop." A little of his previous anger crept back in, and he forced it down, leveling his voice, same as he'd done with Mia last night. He wanted to drive home his point, not drive Hawes away. "You put my people and Kane's in danger today. You put Kane in danger. Because you didn't tell us the whole story. I want it now. I might not deserve your trust, but I deserve that much."

Hawes inhaled deeply, as if centering himself, then effortlessly freed his hand. Chris's control had been sheer illusion in that regard. But Hawes didn't move away. "You're a fed."

"Whatever you say stays between us. I'm not gonna turn you in."

Hawes held his gaze an agonizingly long minute, assessing, before he reclaimed his beer and took a long swig. "I was thinking I was tired of playing defense," he said as he lowered the bottle. "That I wanted to go on offense."

"You were trying to lure them out?" Like Hawes had done with Papa Cal's funeral last week. He'd been tired of waiting then too.

"*Trying* being the operative word. I also needed to test the outside influencer theory."

"The other buyers." Chris had wondered the same thing. "And?"

"Those three weren't involved, which gives me some comfort."

"I saw two enter—cartel and neo-Nazi. Who was the third?"

"Arms dealer who had a unit in the building."

"So you killed the three of them?"

Hawes shrugged. "That gives me comfort too."

"Jesus, Madigan." Chris held his own beer to his forehead, praying for patience and futilely hoping the cold bottle would stem the cresting wave of anger.

"I had contracts on them too."

"Isn't that convenient?"

Hawes cocked a brow. "Are you actually arguing on behalf of a human trafficker, a white supremacist, and an arms dealer, all of whom have threatened our city and escaped justice multiple times?"

Chris drank from his bottle.

One corner of Hawes's sinful mouth quirked up. "Didn't think so." He set his bottle aside, pried Chris's free from his clenched fingers, then stepped closer, only a few inches between them. "I needed to show whoever is behind this grab for power that I know the game they're playing, that I can play it too, and that I'm not afraid to do what it takes to win. That I'll fight for what's mine and for the way I do things." Gone was the ice. His eyes were energized, brimming over with a king's confidence. And heated, the look in them a magnified version of the fire Chris had seen in them yesterday at the BART station. Right after the take-down, right before the too brief kiss.

Chris lifted a hand, wanting desperately to touch, to wallow for a spell in the desire that was pushing away his anger and in the relief that Hawes was safe. And here with him. But what right did he have? Yes, Hawes had initiated the kiss yesterday, but after all that had transpired between them, after Chris's betrayal, he didn't have a right to anything more from Hawes than what he'd given him already. Especially when more was the last thing Chris should be doing.

Hawes didn't give him a choice. He captured Chris's flailing hand and placed it on his waist, encouraging the touch, reestablishing the connection. "I wanted to know who was selling the explosives," he said. "This was the quickest way to getting a shot at that info."

Gliding his hand under the pullover's hem, Chris curled his fingers into warm skin and rubbed his thumb over the jut of Hawes's hip. "You said you weren't using the explosives anymore."

"I didn't."

Chris dropped his hand, forgetting all about Hawes's sharp angles. "Come again?"

"I didn't set those explosives." Righteous indignation flashed across Hawes's face. "I wouldn't risk all those inno-cent residents, or the property manager in the control room, or you, or Brax, or your people. You were wrong about that part." Umbrage gave way to a sly, satisfied smile. "But my plan worked."

"Because the real seller had been there to set those explosives."

Nodding, Hawes erased the inches between them and ran a hand up Chris's chest. "We can figure out the time-line. Maybe their identity. You do your work, and we'll do ours."

"Why'd you tell us about the auction but not the whole story?"

"I took a risk that I could get in and out in time. If the seller had been there when I was, then I would have delivered them to you. I needed law enforcement on-site for that, and in case anything went sideways."

"Did you factor in that they—or we—could've turned the trap on you?"

"I did. Remember that 'I don't trust you' bit..." Hawes cast his gaze aside and stepped back. The magnetic pull between them tugged at Chris's insides, making the absence painful after being close again. Even more so when Hawes turned on his heel and ambled toward the reading nook. He braced an arm over his head, propped against the window casing. "That's why it was only me there."

Chris feared that was the answer, recalling the surveillance footage of Hawes approaching the building alone. Holt had surely been in his ear, but he'd had no on-site backup.

"You would have sacrificed yourself," Chris said as he stopped next to the end of the chaise.

"You wouldn't make that promise, to not sacrifice yourself. And I won't either. If that's what it takes to keep my family and city—you—safe."

"How the fuck am I supposed to argue that, Madigan?"

Hawes rotated and rested against the window. He raised his chin and his eyes, both defiant. "Don't."

Too much confidence and too dark a death wish. Then and now.

Chris closed the distance between them and braced his hands on either side of the window, caging Hawes in. Keeping him close, avoiding the loss that had almost struck today. "Don't keep me in the dark. And don't make me watch you almost die."

Hawes pushed off the window and brought their bodies flush, their lips a breath apart. "I'm just a mark."

"Don't fucking lie either."

Chris made sure he didn't tell any more fibs, crushing their mouths together in a kiss that made words, thoughts, breath impossible. Every bit of desire, relief, frustration, and fear that he'd banked the past four hours, the past four days, was unleashed, driving him to press Hawes back against the window, to run his hands over every sharp angle, to plunge his tongue between Hawes's lips and into his mouth, tasting all that confidence. Tasting the submission when Hawes lifted his arms above his head and clutched either side of the window frame. Open and spread out like he'd been on his condo ladder last week. Hawes needed relief too—from the tightly wound control he'd so expertly wielded today—and Chris wanted to give it to him, wanted that trust back, maybe more than he'd ever wanted anything.

But Chris hesitated, their earlier exchange drifting back

into his mind, a tendril of remorse coiling like Hawes's beloved fog through his veins. Guilt over the lies he'd told. He curled his fingers around Hawes's wrists in a loose grip and leaned their foreheads together. Before he could say anything, though, Hawes rolled his hips and pressed his hard cock against Chris's groin. Chris failed to bite back a groan, and Hawes blinked up at him with lust-darkened eyes.

Eyes that wanted to surrender, but did Hawes understand to whom? Reminded again of his remorse, his guilt, the trust he needed to win back, Chris dragged his hips away and released one of Hawes's wrists. He lowered his hand and cupped Hawes's cheek. Hawes nuzzled his palm, and Chris nearly lost his resolve for good. All that softness under all those sharp angles was like a lasso around every tender part of Chris, hopelessly ensnaring him.

The satisfying snap of a puzzle piece into place.

He rubbed his thumb over Hawes's lovely, sharp jawline, waiting for Hawes to lift his eyes again. "Are you sure about this?" He squeezed Hawes's wrist still in his hand against the glass. There was no mistaking his question. "Before, you gave this to someone I wasn't, and I'm sorry for that."

Hawes snaked his free hand around Chris's neck and into the hair at his nape. Fingers splayed, he combed outward and forced the tie out of Chris's hair, freeing his topknot. "You said I could trust you." He raked his fingers through the long strands, making Chris shiver. "It wasn't all a lie, was it?"

"You can, and it wasn't." Chris sighed softly, helplessly. "Fuck, Hawes, most of it was true, but I'm sorry, so very sorry, for the parts that weren't."

Conflicting emotions, too many to dissect, raced across Hawes's face, flowed out to his fingers that clenched in Chris's hair, then combusted. Hawes melted under him, and Chris held him up with his body, pressed between him and the glass again. "I'm sorry too," Hawes whispered hoarsely. "For not telling you the truth."

"You had your reasons."

He cleared his throat. "I knew the risks today, owned them, did what I had to do for my family, my city." He untangled his fingers from Chris's hair and lifted his arm back into position, mirroring the other. "Now I need to let go, *for me*. That's why I'm here. I want to do that *with you*. I need to."

Leaving Hawes's arms raised, Chris ran his hands down their toned length, across Hawes's broad chest that led to a tapered waist, then under his pullover and thin T-shirt. He splayed his hands across Hawes's cool skin and ribbed abs, then skirted them over his hips and down inside the waistband of his jeans. His ass cheeks were cool from the window and gloriously firm and round, filling Chris's hands. He hauled Hawes forward with a grunt and ground their cocks together. "How the fuck am I supposed to argue that?" Argue any of it.

White-knuckling the window frame, Hawes used his abs, like he did when he'd lifted his lower body off the bed on Friday, to do that again now, circling Chris's waist with his legs, capturing him, locking them together. "Same answer. Don't."

Chris conceded and stole back into Hawes's mouth, until other needs became pressing. As much as he loved the lithe, powerful body trapped between him and the window, loved Hawes's cock rutting against his abs, loved every nook and cranny of Hawes's mouth he reacquainted himself with, he loved the thought of a naked Hawes more. And this position was not conducive to making his thoughts a reality.

Hands around Hawes's wrists, Chris brought their arms down behind Hawes's back. Following the cue, Hawes bowed his back and thrust his chest forward, more of his weight onto Chris. "On three."

Chris skipped one and two. "Three," he said, and hauled them off the window. Spinning, he took two steps and put a knee to the chaise. He laid Hawes against the corner, spreading his arms across the top of the chaise and his legs half on and half off the seat cushions, wide enough for Chris to crawl between them.

Hawes nestled into the cushions and smiled. "Definitely softer than the window."

"Wanna know what's not soft?" Chris palmed his cock through his jeans, stretching denim across his thickening length.

Hawes's smile morphed into a wanton growl. "Bring it to me."

Chris nearly caved at Hawes's desperation-soaked command. Could see himself feeding Hawes his cock, could imagine how good the rumble of his groan would feel around the tip. But not yet. "We'll get there," he promised, getting back to the task of undressing.

He ran his hands under Hawes's pullover and shirt and slowly worked them up his torso, torturing with tongue and teeth every inch of skin he exposed. "When we're done here," he said between licks and kisses, "I want you to stay."

"I can't." Hawes gasped as Chris barely breathed on a nipple. "I need to—"

"Fall asleep in my bed tonight." Chris wanted it as much as he wanted to get his mouth around Hawes's cock. "Fall asleep in my arms again, here in my home, with me." Maybe even more, after the events of today. "I need that after almost losing you." He took a nipple between his teeth, and Hawes arched his back. "After almost losing this."

Hawes kept his arms spread across the top of the chaise, fingers digging into the cushions as his body writhed for contact. "Yes. I'll stay."

Chris's chest clenched as he was reminded of the hole there that had been filled again. He amped up the torture as a thank-you, as a promise. He held his body above Hawes's and focused all his efforts on a single point of contact, his tongue swirling around one, then the other of Hawes's nipples. They puckered and strained like the rest of Hawes's body. Like Chris's to match.

Unable to resist Hawes's "Need to feel you" pleas any longer, he made quick work of getting their shirts off. He lowered himself on top of Hawes—chest to chest, skin to skin, mouth to mouth—and lost himself in kisses, in touches, in softness. Except their cocks, which grew harder as they rutted together with increasing urgency.

Chris braced one foot on the floor and bent his other leg between Hawes's spread legs, knee on the cushion. "The other night on the phone, I was here on this chaise." He unbuttoned Hawes's jeans and tugged them down with his boxers, enough to set his cock bobbing free. Chris stretched back out over Hawes, whispering hotly into his ear, "Your voice…" He wrapped a fist around Hawes's hard length and stroked slowly. "Made me so hard, like you are now."

"Dante…"

"Thought about you spread out just like this." Another stroke. "Wanted to taste you again." A swipe of his fingers over the leaking head. "Suck you down until you let go."

Hawes keened for more, his arms slipping off the back of the chaise. Chris released his cock and grabbed each wrist, spreading them back across the cushion tops. "Keep 'em there, and hold on tight while I take you apart."

He slid to his knees beside the chaise and yanked Hawes's jeans and boxers the rest of the way off. Chris bent over his lap and licked a stripe up the crease of Hawes's balls. As intended, Hawes lifted his ass off the chaise, chasing the touch, and Chris gave it to him. He shoved a hand back to tease Hawes's taint and hole, while the other fisted the base of Hawes's cock. His mouth swallowed him down, teasing and tasting. Sharp, irresistible, like the rest of Hawes.

"Fucking hell," Hawes cursed. "I'm not gonna last if you keep that up."

"And I'm not gonna last when I get my cock in your mouth." Chris kissed down Hawes's length as he spoke. "Gotta make sure you're ready to go with me." Then took him back into his mouth.

Lost in the perfect, aching hardness, in his mouth and in his own jeans, it wasn't until Hawes shouted, "Christopher!" that Chris came back to himself. And to Hawes staring down at him with eyes that were nearly black, the blue reduced to a thin ring of icy fire. "Get your cock in me now, one way or the other."

Chris almost came at the delicious snap of command in

Hawes's voice. Driven wild, he had to act before it was too late. He stood, stepped back, and shed his jeans and boxers. He took another step back, and Hawes opened his mouth to object, but Chris circled the chaise, stopping behind the corner were Hawes's head was, and Hawes caught on to his fantasy.

His objection died on a groan. "Oh fuck yes."

Chris ran a hand through Hawes's silky top strands, tipping his head back. With his other hand, he moved one of Hawes's off the back of the chaise to the patch of hair just above Hawes's cock, urging him to take himself in hand. "Together," he said.

Hawes grinned and slid his hand down, circling his cock. "Don't think that's gonna be a problem."

Neither did Chris as he fisted the base of his own cock and fed it between Hawes's parted lips. Deciding where to look became almost as hard as his cock—Hawes's fist shuttling up and down that lovely, slick cock, or his lips stretching around Chris's length, his cheeks hollowing out with suction.

"Christ." Chris curled forward, tangling the fingers of his free hand with Hawes's on top of the cushions. Hawes clutched back, hard. This wasn't going to last long for either of them.

Hawes took him deeper each time Chris thrust forward, throat tightening around the tip as he swallowed, tongue twirling around the length and head as Chris drew back. "Oh fuck, that's it. That's perfect." It was the hottest fuck Chris had ever had, and if the orgasm barreling his way was any indication, it was going to be the hardest he'd ever come too. "Hawes…" He started to pull out, but the fingers around his clenched to almost breaking.

Commanding him to stay. With him.

Chris knew exactly where to look. Knew exactly whose order to follow.

His king's.

He thrust back into Hawes's mouth, ecstasy trilling up his spine with Hawes's deep, satisfied groan as they came, together.

ELEVEN

Chris followed the scent of coffee out from his bedroom, the condo still in shadows, the dark of night outside just starting to give way to morning. Inside, the under-cabinet lights cast a soft glow in the kitchen, and across from the island, another low light emanated from the study.

While they'd fallen asleep in the same bed, Hawes wrapped in his arms, as negotiated, Hawes had beaten him awake and was snooping around the locked study he'd picked his way into, judging by the bent wire on the kitchen island. Not that there was anything in the room that wasn't on the flash drive Chris had already given him.

He leaned a shoulder against the doorjamb and admired the graceful, efficient motions of his lover. Dressed in his jeans and one of Chris's tanks, Hawes looked at home here, with his feet bare, his hair tumbled, and a mug of coffee in hand. He was the first person since Izzy to invade his space —his life—so effortlessly, so comfortably. It should worry him that it was Hawes Madigan, of all people, but it was the first time in years he didn't feel alone in his own home.

And that's what it felt like for the first time in years too—a home. The pieces all fit, even if they shouldn't.

"You didn't look around last night?" he asked after another minute of creeping on the handsome, dangerous man.

Hawes didn't startle, no doubt aware that Chris had been standing there, staring. "Needed the beer, and the sex." He grinned over his shoulder, but then the smile fell as he considered the photos of Isabella's crime scene. "Was still shook up from the almost dying."

"You hid it well."

"Not the first time." He swung his gaze back to Chris. "We're professionals."

"We are."

Hawes got that about him and vice versa. Maybe that's why Hawes didn't feel like a stranger in his home. Chris pushed off the jamb, ambled over to him, and slid an arm around his waist. "Doesn't make it any easier, does it? Risking your life on a daily basis is still risking your life."

Hawes set his mug on the desk, then turned into Chris, warm hand on his bare chest. The other curled around the waistband of his athletic shorts and tugged Chris closer. "You do, though. You steady things. I don't know why…"

"You do too, for me." Chris didn't know why either, only knew that he needed to kiss Hawes, needed to taste him this morning, unlike the last morning they'd woken up in the same place yet on opposite sides. Chris mapped every sweet, delicious corner of his mouth while Hawes mapped every inch of Chris's back and torso, sending ripples of heat coursing under his skin, through his veins, aimed straight for the center of his chest. When air became necessary again, Hawes rested against his chest, and Chris combed fingers through his wild morning hair. "Find anything interesting?"

"You have a lovely home."

Chris chuckled. "For an ATF agent."

Hawes leaned back in his arms. "I didn't say that."

"Didn't have to." Chris dropped a quick kiss on his lips, then stepped out of Hawes's arms. He grabbed Hawes's empty mug and headed for the kitchen to refill it for him and grab his own. "It needs some updates," he said as he ran a hand over the countertops. Chipped in places, grout an indescribable color, the tiles themselves a nineties off-white that never looked clean even if he scrubbed them to gleaming. "But I'm not a fool. I know the goldmine I'm sitting on. Bought it fifteen years ago before prices went crazy. It's almost doubled in value since."

"You thinking about selling it? If you're not here much…"

"I primarily work UC. I'm gone a lot." He pulled down another mug. "But I'm not planning to sell anytime soon. It's not exactly lived in, not like it used to be, but I like having a place of my own when I am here. My four walls, not my mom's or my sister's."

"I understand that." Hawes circled the adjacent dining table, eyeing the books scattered haphazardly across it. "And you have to have somewhere to keep all these."

"I like to read."

Hawes stepped away from the dining table and laid a hand on the hallway wall between Chris's bedroom and the study. "That a hidden library in here? Or a panic room? There's no door here or on the study side."

"You didn't try to open the door in the bedroom?"

"It seemed private." Chris rolled his eyes, hard, and

Hawes dropped his hand, chuckling. "More private than the other areas."

Chris smiled as he filled their mugs. "It's nothing quite so fancy." He handed Hawes a refreshed cup. "It's storage now, but it was a nursery."

Hawes bobbled the mug, and Chris, hand still close by, expecting the reaction, helped him steady it. "A what?" Hawes said.

Chris hadn't planned on telling Hawes this truth quite yet, but after yesterday, Hawes needed to know the truth, all of it, so he could understand where Chris was coming from, why he'd made the decisions he had, why losing Hawes wasn't an option, and why solving Isabella's death was at the top of his priority ladder. Chris grabbed his own mug, took Hawes's hand with the other, and led him back to the reading area. He beckoned Hawes to sit on the chaise, handed him his coffee, and turned to the bookcase. He pulled the single hardcover book—*Where the Wild Things Are*—off the top shelf, where he'd put it back after his conversation with Mia, and carefully flipped the pages until he reached the photo tucked inside. He withdrew it and held it out to Hawes.

Perched on the end of the chaise, Hawes set the mugs on the floor and took the offered photo. He ran his finger over the kindergartner's face and smiled, much like he did anytime he looked at Lily. He'd make an incredible father someday. "Is this your niece? She looks like you. Same dark eyes and dark hair." He ran his thumb over the nose and laughed. "Even the nose. Did she stay with you?"

"That's not my niece. Mia is incapable of smiling at a camera. That"—he nodded at the picture—"was my daughter, Rochelle."

Hawes gasped. "Daughter? You have—Wait, *was*?"

Chris lowered himself next to Hawes and slipped the picture from his trembling fingers. "Ro would have been seventeen this coming December." He smiled at the photo of his beaming daughter on school picture day.

"You had her in high school?"

"Well, I didn't have her, technically." His smile dimmed, remembering her first cry, imagining her last. "Don't have her anymore either."

Hawes gently squeezed his knee. "Dante..." Then squeezed tighter. "Shit, Chris, I'm sorry. That's..."

Chris laid a hand over his, drawing Hawes's gaze. "I like when you call me Dante." He placed the picture of Ro on the side table, then retrieved their mugs off the floor. He handed one to Hawes, then scooted behind him into the corner of the chaise, a leg on either side of Hawes, who took the hint and repositioned himself, back to Chris's chest.

"You remember Jennifer Petrie?" Chris asked once they were settled.

"The cheerleader from the yearbook?"

"That's the one. Knocked her up the night of senior prom."

"And she had Rochelle."

Chris took a long sip of the perfectly brewed coffee and remembered those wild months of his eighteen-year-old life, wishing he'd had an IV drip of caffeine then. Jenn's panic when she came to him with the news, his mother's glee and support, his own fear, and then something so much more the day his daughter was born. "The reason I was so sure Holt was the traitor was because I know how he feels. To have your whole world suddenly realign and revolve around this new life. One you'd do anything to protect. That was Ro for me."

"And Jennifer?"

"Wanted to do right by Ro, but we weren't in love, and she had no interest in being a mom yet. She had a scholarship to Florida and a shitty family at home. She needed to get out, for her own safety and future."

"Whereas you had your mom, dad, and sister."

"I had the support network to make it work, like Holt has all of you. And I had a job working on bikes with my dad at the family shop and a spot at San Francisco State. I was in a better position to care for Ro." He cleared his throat, and when that didn't dislodge the knot there, gulped back more coffee. "She was my whole world the second she first wailed."

Hawes twisted in his arms to look up at him. "You don't have to…"

Chris leaned forward and nuzzled the hollow of his cheek. "You need this piece of the story." Hawes nodded, and Chris settled back into the corner, Hawes against his chest again. "I graduated with a degree in criminal justice and became a private investigator."

"So you really were a PI?"

He draped an arm around Hawes's chest and squeezed. "Told you it wasn't all a lie." Hawes chuffed and dipped his chin to nip at Chris's forearm. Improbably laughing, Chris left his arm there, lightly holding Hawes, enjoying the feel of him in his embrace and steeling himself for the hardest part of the story. "PI work paid well, and with some help from my parents, I bought this place. The job gave me more flexibility to be at home here, with my kid."

"Sounds ideal."

"It was a good setup, and the PI gig was how I met Isabella." Hawes tensed in his arms, then relaxed when Chris tightened his hold, comforting them both. "I was running down a lead on a firearm when I first crossed paths with her. We worked well together—both of us getting what we needed for our respective cases—and then we went our separate ways."

"Until something happened to Ro? You said Isabella helped you at a time when you weren't in a good way."

The mug began to shake in Chris's hand, and he leaned down to set it on the floor. Righting himself, Chris found his hand captured in Hawes's, their fingers lacing together, giving him the strength he needed to go on. "My sister had picked her daughter and Ro up from school. Drunk driver ran a red light less than a block from the house. He died, and so did…" Chris lost his words, and Hawes raised their joined hands, kissing across the knuckles until Chris could speak again. "The rest of my family was okay, but Ro didn't make it."

Hawes rotated so his side rested against the length of Chris's torso, his breath gentle where it coasted over Chris's skin. "Take your time."

There'd never be enough time to digest that loss, all the feelings wrapped up in it. Chris carded his fingers through Hawes's hair instead, taking comfort where he could, short-lived as it was. "You need to go," he said after another minute. "Before it gets light out."

"It's fine," Hawes replied. "Tell me the rest."

The whip of an order underlying the gentle tone was enough of a distraction from the sorrow. Chris smiled as he cleared his throat. "I barely made it too. My whole world was gone. I was ready to join her. I used one of my connections to get hold of a gun."

"You didn't have one?"

"I did, but I wanted it clean. Untraceable so no one would be implicated but me. That's what I told myself, and it was stupid. Years of therapy later, I understand what I wanted was to be stopped."

"And that's where Isabella came in."

"The gun I'd bought wasn't clean. She had it tagged for a case. I was five minutes from pulling the trigger when she walked in." He remembered that day, would never forget it. At the end of a dark tunnel, literally and figuratively as he sat in the dark in this very room, when the tall, bossy lady with a mane of black curls and a thick New York accent came looking for him. "More like strutted in, to this very house, and rather than trying to coax or offer sympathy, she dropped a file on the floor in front of me. For a seven-year-old girl being held captive by a cult."

"Smart," Hawes said. "You couldn't save Ro, but you could save the other girl."

"Izzy was recruiting me. She gave me a purpose." He gently pushed Hawes up, wanting to see his face for this part, or rather, wanting Hawes to see his. This was too important. "Which is why I can't let her killer go. I couldn't avenge Ro's death, but I can avenge Izzy's. I have to."

Hawes stiffened in his arms one second and vaulted out of them the next, rocketing off the chaise like he'd been burned. Chris caught his wrist before he could shut down and put Chris out of reach again. "Hey, what's wrong?"

"Nothing." Hawes cast his gaze down, then at the bookcase, then out the window. Anywhere but at Chris.

Not nothing. Chris ran a thumb over the inside of

Hawes's wrist, the racing pulse point there thrumming under his fingertip. "You've known all along that finding Izzy's killer is my primary mission. The ATF has me on the explosives, but I won't drop this until I find out what really happened to my partner. I wanted you to understand why it matters."

"I did. I do." Hawes swallowed hard but still wouldn't look at him. "It matters to me too," he said, barely a whisper.

Chris believed him. The changes Hawes had made in the organization since the night of Izzy's death were proof. So why wasn't he proud of them? Why did he always tense when Chris brought up finding her killer? Unless he knew more than he was letting on, in which case… "Who are you protect—"

Noise from outside cut off Chris's words. Louder than the usual critters, but not so loud that it would wake the neighbors. If both he and Hawes weren't trained as they were, they may not have heard it either. But they were, and they did.

Chris cursed. "My gun's in the safe." He started to let go of Hawes's hand, to head for his bedroom safe, or if there wasn't enough time, to the kitchen knives, but Hawes reversed their grip, grasping his wrist and halting him mid-stride.

"Hold a second," he whispered, on alert but not tensed to battle-ready. Before Chris could ask what he was on about, a set of knocks rapped below the window. Hawes's form relaxed, and he dropped Chris's hand. "I invited them." He crossed to the back door as footsteps started up the stairs. He opened the door, and Holt and Helena entered, Lily in her aunt's arms for a change.

Chris thought to object—they all knew where he lived now—but Holt had figured that much out already and given Hawes the address. At least Hawes had invited them, unlike at Hawes's condo, where they barged in unannounced on the regular. A heads-up would have been nice, but Chris hadn't given Hawes a chance, having jumped right into the history lesson.

On cue, the baby in Helena's arms wailed her disapproval of the rising sun, and Chris couldn't help but smile. "You got a microwave in this place?" Helena asked. "Bottle time."

Chris held an arm out toward the kitchen, and the troop of Madigans made themselves at home. Holt set up at the bar, computer open, Hawes got another pot of coffee brewing, and Helena dug a bottle out of the baby bag and stuck the bottle in the microwave.

That done, she rotated and leaned back against the counter, surveying the space. "Nice place, Mr. Hair."

"Glad it meets your approval." He circled the end of the island, opened the junk drawer, and fished out a folded Post-it. He slid it across the bar to Holt. "In case you need the wireless password."

Holt's tired, dark eyes flicked from the faded neon slip of paper, to the drawer Chris had pulled it from, to Chris. He looked more like himself again, albeit still weary. "I wouldn't connect to your system." He withdrew a hot spot from the baby bag and plugged it into the laptop. "I'm not an idiot."

The snarky judgment made Chris laugh. "Of course not." Ice broken, he lowered his voice and said to Holt, "You didn't tell him about Ro." He was sure Holt must have turned up that info in his revised search.

Holt's eyes tracked to his daughter, to Chris, then back to the screen. "Not my story to tell."

"Thank you." Smiling, Chris moved the rest of the way around the island to the fridge and pulled out the creamer, readying it for when Hawes passed out steaming mugs of coffee.

Holt gulped back half of his, then spun his laptop around so they could all see the screen. "This was the tip we received this morning."

Chris scalded his throat in his haste to swallow. "What tip?"

Hawes gestured at the screen. "This is why I invited them here."

Chris leaned forward and read the email. "The seller made contact..." He looked over his shoulder at Helena. "With you?"

"With me." Her expression was deadly serious, even as she fed Lily her bottle and patted her bottom. "They're offering me a chance to buy back the explosives."

Chris shifted his gaze to Hawes. "Why are you bringing this to me now?"

"We kept you on the sidelines yesterday," Hawes said. "That was a mistake, and it almost didn't work out. We need to coordinate. I won't have those explosives loose in my city."

"So your play worked," Chris said, satisfied that their interests were aligned. "They're on the defensive and trying to pick off the pass."

Hawes sipped from his mug. "Likely."

"Could this be Amelia?"

"Possibly," Holt answered. "She knows how to disguise

the IP address. But we told Brax not to give her access to a computer."

"I called him," Helena told them. "Confirmed it. No access to any mobile devices either."

"So she told someone how to do this, then," Chris said. "Or they have another hacker, and this plan was on her flash drive. Any luck there yet?"

Holt shook his head.

"But she can vet the tip," Hawes said. "She can tell us if this was part of the plan, fallback or otherwise."

Or lead Hawes right where her faction wanted him. "It's a trap," Chris said.

"That's what I told him," Helena said, and Holt nodded too.

Hawes finished his mug and set it in the sink. "We all agree on that point. Now, how do we turn the trap back around on them? Because I am done with this shit."

Chris tilted his head toward the study, and the lot of them followed him in. Helena whistled low and handed Lily off to Holt, who grumbled under his breath about "too much fucking paper." Chris chuckled as he walked over to the org chart. "They've wiped out your lieutenants, and two of your soldiers are in custody."

"They?" Hawes said, hip against the desk, arms folded over his chest.

"One of them." Chris pointed at the layer of captains.

Hawes shook his head. "We don't think so. Alibis check out. Half aren't even here. They're out on contracts."

Chris rested a hand next to the X adjacent to the chart. "Then someone out here."

"The competition," Helena said. "We were thinking that already."

The reason they'd set up the trap at the building yesterday.

"Three of which are gone," Holt added.

"I have my ideas," Hawes said, then glanced at Helena. "We need to talk to Rose. There could be older players we're not familiar with who are looking to exploit the perceived power vacuum."

"Get a list from her, and then I can see if they crossed paths with…" Holt's words drifted off, and he stared out the front window, holding Lily closer.

It had been a nice reprieve—the siblings firing on all cylinders, a sight and process that fascinated Chris—until reality reentered the picture. Hawes moved to his brother's side and squeezed his arm.

"Be sure you look back three years," Chris said, keeping them focused. "To the night—"

Hawes's gaze shot to him, but it was Helena who spoke. "To the night your partner died."

"Was murdered." Three pale faces stared back at him as he rapped his knuckles against the wall between the X and the org chart. "I'd bet my badge that this person, whoever they are, was responsible for Izzy's death."

"And what are you going to do to them?" Hawes said.

"Find out who they are, and then we spring the trap."

An awkward few seconds of silence followed before Lily broke it with a wail. "We need to get her home for a nap," Holt said.

Helena kicked into action, moving back into the kitchen to pack up their bags, Holt on her heels. Hawes, however, stood frozen, gaze whipping back and forth between the wall of crime scene photos and his siblings. Was he imagining them there? Or himself? They'd all been in the line of fire this past week, intentionally and not.

"Hey," Chris said softly, stepping close and cupping Hawes's cheek. He waited for blue eyes to meet his, then rested their foreheads together. "We won't let anything happen to them. And I won't let anything happen to you."

"Thank you." He leaned forward and captured Chris's mouth, stealing his breath and heart in a stunning kiss, one that said more than their words or previous kisses ever had, including a confounding trace of *goodbye*.

TWELVE

Up early owing to his overnight and morning visitors, Chris beat most of the agents and staff into the office. All but one. Light shined from under the partially closed war-room door, and strains of The Grateful Dead floated out into the otherwise quiet space. Of course Wheeler had pulled an all-nighter. Chris didn't expect anything less from him.

He didn't, however, expect the decent choice in music from someone so uptight. Nor did he expect to push the door the rest of the way open and find the other agent facedown on his files, asleep. Coat, tie, and vest folded neatly over one of the other chairs, Wheeler had his wrinkled dress sleeves rolled up and his head pillowed on his folded arms. He continued to snore lightly, undisturbed by Chris's entrance. For Wheeler to be that dead to the world, he'd probably only recently fallen asleep. Chris surveyed the rest of the room, confirming his suspicion. Wheeler had been at this all night from the impressive look of it. The whiteboard of notes behind him was impossibly more packed with sharp, slanted scribble, and at the other end of the room, the flip board was now covered in photos, plans, and notes from yesterday's scene.

Chris skirted behind Wheeler, turning down the music and flicking the coffee maker on as he walked to the other end of the room. He stood before the board, arms crossed, examining what Wheeler had pieced together. Building schematics. Before and after shots of the buyer rooms and the destroyed ventilation unit on the roof above them, where the explosion had originated. Charred remains of the three buyers. The trigger device in the stairwell. The heat signatures showing the path Hawes had run, room to room, killing his targets. Ferrying bids, as far as Wheeler knew. Surveillance photos from the hour time window before and after the explosion, a red circle drawn on two of them—by Wheeler, Chris presumed—around the head of a man Chris didn't recognize. Hawes with his head held high as he entered the building, then with his face covered in soot and a child in his arms as he later emerged next to Kane.

A chill snaked up Chris's spine, as he was reminded again of how close he'd come to losing everything he'd worked on for the past three years and everything he'd found the past week.

As the scent of stale coffee began to waft around him, Chris rested back against the table, examining the evidence from a thirty-five-thousand-foot level. Trying to assess how and when the seller had infiltrated and set the explosives. On the schematics, another red circle was drawn over a set of sub-sidewalk basement doors and a red line led from there to a utility closet inside the building. Right next to the north stairwell. Could that be the access route they were looking for? Was the man in the photos the person who traveled the path?

Per the debrief yesterday, Jax was gathering surveillance from the time period between when the Madigans had posted the auction ad to the time of the blast. The ATM had only been clicked on that afternoon, but there were traffic cams and other sources they could maybe pull useful footage from. Get a lock on who had come and gone from the building. Had the stranger been there another time? Chris withdrew his phone, snapped pictures of the photos and the schematics, and shot them off with a text to Kane and Jax, suggesting they refocus their surveillance back-track to the indicated location with an eye for this person.

"I'm sorry about yesterday."

Chris dropped his phone into his pocket and rotated toward the voice.

Upright, Wheeler scrubbed both hands over his face and into his hair, doing a terrible job of taming it. "You were right. We could have lost agents, but I was too busy trying to get the bust to end all busts." He slumped back in the chair and dropped his hands into his lap. "I wasn't going about it the right way."

Add another check in the impressed column. An agent who could admit when he was wrong, who could adjust and learn, was a valuable asset. Chris mentally added two checks, since Wheeler was also taking on more of the blame than he deserved in this case. But he couldn't tell him that.

"It happens," he said instead. "And we didn't lose any agents."

"We're still waiting on an ID on the third body."

Chris couldn't tell him who that was either, not without

letting on the full truth of yesterday's incident. "But all our agents and all of Kane's officers are accounted for, yes?"

"Yes, thankfully. We assume it was another buyer, given the location. We'll see who else turns up in the surveillance. Match it against dental, if we can salvage that much."

"ME say how long?"

"Couple days, if there are dental records."

Not likely. He needed to get that ID to Wheeler some other way before it served as another point of distraction. Or led Wheeler somewhere Chris didn't want him to go. "Pull the resident records," Chris said. "Let's see if there was anyone already in the building who could be a buyer."

"We already did that," Wheeler said. "Before the bust."

"Check it against aliases." He tapped the photos of the stranger. "And against this guy you circled. Do we know who he is?"

Wheeler shook his head. "No, but other than general databases, I didn't have much to go on other than my gut, which tells me he might be one of the heat signatures in the north stairwell just before the explosion."

"You might be right. Let's see if he's a resident or connected to one."

Wheeler held his gaze, searching, and Chris worried he'd given away too much, but then Wheeler leaned forward and opened his laptop, shooting off an email. While he did that, Chris filled a mug, set the coffee next to Wheeler, then rounded the table to sit across from him.

"Thank you," Wheeler said before taking a sip and grimacing. "I thought y'all were supposed to have good coffee in this town."

It was the first slip of Southern accent Chris had detected from the Georgia-born agent, and the twangy word, along with the observation, made him chuckle. "Have you been in many ATF offices that have good coffee?"

"Touché."

"You want good coffee, raid the FBI's stash. The SAC is a coffee snob."

"Good to know." He took another long swallow, face pinching slightly less this time, then lowered the mug, hands still wrapped around it. His gaze drifted to the Madigan org chart. "You know these people better than anyone. I should have listened to you." Then drifted back to Chris. "The explosives are our objective."

Assured of Wheeler's redirected focus, Chris withdrew the piece of paper from his inner coat pocket and slid it across the table. "You'll have another chance. Friday."

Wheeler's eyes grew wide as he read the email to Helena. "How did you get this?"

"Doesn't matter."

Skeptical brown eyes shot to his. "Perri…"

"Do you want to secure the explosives?"

Their stare-down lasted a good ten seconds before Wheeler finally nodded. Chris slowly let his held breath out through his nose.

"Good," he said. "You're going to spec out this strike. We don't know where yet, rolling location, so it's going to be complicated. We need to consider all possible locations and have contingencies ready. I'll coordinate with the Madigans." His eyes flickered to the picture of Hawes and back. Wheeler nodded again. "And I'll add what I know to the mission planning, after I vet the tip."

"Vet it with whom?" Wheeler asked.

"Amelia Madigan."

By the time Chris made it to SFPD headquarters, Kane was well on his way to pacing a hole through the floor outside the interrogation rooms. Tie askew, top button of his dress shirt undone, bags under his eyes, and deep creases at the corners of his drawn mouth, the chief looked to be living the longest twenty-four hours—longest two weeks—of his life. Chris was sure it was nothing compared to Kane's time in the military, but family had a way of complicating matters.

"The arraignment?" Chris asked, worried something else had gone off the rails. Seemed to be their luck lately.

Kane paused in his circuit and ran a hand over his head. "As well as it could go. Bail denied. Flight risk."

"I'm sure all those pictures of her at the offshore bank helped."

"That and a slush fund north of ten million that Holt found last night."

That explained why Hawes's brother had seemed both more engaged and more worn down this morning. He'd had a successful hack and found the last thing he'd wanted.

"Any luck tracing the funds?"

Kane resumed his pacing. "He's working on it."

Chris leaned against the wall, out of his way. "Amelia still tight-lipped?"

"Relatively."

"Probably gonna make this harder."

"Tell me what's going on before we walk in there," Kane said. "No more of this getting blindsided shit."

"Someone reached out to Helena offering to broker a sale."

Kane's steps faltered, and his eyes grew wide. "For when?"

"Friday. But I need Amelia to vet it."

"Are we sure this tip is—Wait, that's why Helena called to confirm Amelia hadn't accessed any devices?"

Chris nodded. "Which makes me fairly certain that, yes, this is a legit tip," he said, reading where Kane's previous question had been going. This wasn't a Madigan-engineered setup like yesterday. "We need Amelia to confirm it's from the right outside party. Not from someone else trying to insert themselves into the feud for their own gain."

"Might not be as hard as you think," Kane said. "Holt and Lily were in the courtroom today." He stopped and stared at the interrogation room door, empathy swirling in his hazel eyes. "She misses her daughter, and I think she even regrets betraying Holt. But the judge didn't give her a chance to say that or visit with them. Just ordered her back to solitary lock-up as soon as we're done here, until the present threat has passed."

As a parent, Chris had an inkling of what Amelia must feel. Knew well that tug of the heart demanding you do anything to get back to your kid. He felt that everyday about Ro, still, but there was no getting back to her. She was gone. But Lily wasn't, and neither was Amelia, and if there was one thing Chris didn't doubt, it was that Amelia loved her daughter. She might have lost sight of that temporarily, or interpreted her actions as being taken out of love, but as a new mother, this had to be killing her.

Which gave them leverage. "If we can change that…"

"Exactly," Kane said. "Give her the thing she wants most."

Chris didn't think it was power anymore. He hoped it wasn't, or this strategy—the only one they had—would backfire.

He entered the interrogation room and slid into the chair beside Kane, across from Amelia and her counsel. One look at Nurse Madigan, and Chris upgraded their chances. Kane was right. Her posture and manner were stoic, but her eyes and nose were red, her dress hung loose on her willowy frame, and she kept her hands clasped in a fist in front of her, as if trying to hold in the trembles that rippled out over the rest of her body.

"Did you always know who I was?" Chris asked. That question had been gnawing at him since the weekend. How much of a pawn had he been? "Or did you just figure it out last week?"

Amelia's green eyes flickered to Kane, then back.

"Cat's out of the bag," Chris said, answering her silent question.

Her clasped hands relaxed a measure. "Guess that explains why you weren't at the arraignment."

"And who exactly are you?" her lawyer asked.

Oakland Ashe, or "Oak" as Kane had greeted him, was a handsome man by any objective standard—dark hair, gray eyes, trim, fit body for a man in his mid-forties—and all of him was expensive. From his three-figure haircut to his tailored suit, to his shiny shoes, to the diamond-encrusted wedding band on his ring finger and the matching gold-and-diamond Rolex on his wrist. The Madigans had spared no expense getting Amelia the best. And he was earning his paycheck.

Chris dug his badge out of his back pocket and tossed it onto the table. "Special Agent Christopher Perri. ATF."

Oak picked up the badge and examined his credentials. "You're the agent from the incident at Hawes's loft?" At Chris's nod, Oak closed the billfold and sent it skidding back across the table to him. "My client doesn't have to answer that question if it will incriminate her."

"More than she already is?"

Oak opened his mouth to object, but Chris cut him off. "She's got enough charges to deal with. I'm not looking to add more. I'm just looking for some backstory." He turned his attention to Amelia. "My goal is not to get you more time in jail, but less."

Amelia couldn't hide her full-body tremor. "Less?" Or the lilt of hope in her voice.

Kane was right. They could use this.

"Ms. Madigan, you—"

Amelia waved Oak off. "Yes, I knew who you were before you showed up last week."

"Because your boss told you?"

"They did."

The gender-neutral pronoun gave nothing away. Her caginess, however, did. "Amelia, if you're protecting someone…"

"I'm protecting my family."

"By setting them up to take this hit?"

"Not all of them."

Just Hawes. Consistent with her actions and those of her faction last week. They didn't want to take the whole empire down. Only remove the king. "Is that why someone reached out to Helena?" He withdrew the copy of the email and pushed it across the table. "Is she your boss's backup plan or the ultimate goal?"

Surprise flashed across her face for the second time in as many minutes. "Helena almost shot me. You saw that with your own eyes."

"Oh, I don't think she's your ally," Chris said, convinced now that the siblings wouldn't turn on each other. No, this was someone else's doing. "But your boss is moving all of us around on the board, and it looks like they cut you loose in favor of the other sister. The real one."

It was a low blow, but had the intended effect. Amelia's shoulders slumped, and her gulp was audible.

"Amelia," Kane said, voice gentler, playing the good cop. They'd been friends once, and he was the known quantity here. "We're trying to protect them too."

She turned soft, too seeing eyes on Kane. "I know you are, Brax. But you're both so far out of your league."

"Are we at least on the same field with this?" Chris nudged the sheet of paper. "Is it from your boss? Was this the plan?"

Her eyes glided back to him, less soft, more amused and calculating. "Who's left, if not Helena?"

"I need more to vet this."

"Vet," she scoffed, her demeanor changing again on a dime. "You sound like him already. Everything has to be *vetted*. You're adjusting your frame of reference the wrong direction. We're all here because of the one night it all changed, the one night he didn't vet something."

The one night it all changed.

Chris was right. This was all connected to that night three years ago. "The organization didn't vet who Isabella really was," he said, tying it together. "Did you know that too? Is that why she was murdered?"

"Ms. Madigan—"

"Don't worry, Oak," Amelia replied, even though her eyes stayed locked on Chris. "I know better than to answer that one."

"Anything you can do to help us will factor into sentencing," Kane redirected, getting them back on track. "We don't want to take you away from Lily. She needs her mother."

As fast as the fight had resurged in Amelia, she deflated, reminded of what was really at stake here. Her shoulders curled forward, her chin dipped, and tears pooled in her eyes.

"Please, Amelia," Kane urged.

"Yes," she said quietly. "We always intended to recruit Helena."

"But earlier when we showed you the email," Chris said, "you were surprised."

"That they're doing it so soon."

"Did you actually think it would work? That she'd betray her brothers?"

"Me, no," Amelia said. "But they're running out of time."

Because Hawes's plan had worked. "They're spooked."

"It would appear so," Amelia said. "Maybe we misjudged you. And him."

Same as Chris had done. "Lot of that going around."

THIRTEEN

From the outside, across the intersection at Hyde and Beach, it looked like any other Wednesday night at the Buena Vista. Red neon sign lit out front, yellow globe lights casting the interior of the old haunt in a warm, soft glow, a smattering of patrons on stools at the ornate wooden bar and at the low, round tables, most of them sipping the Irish coffees the establishment was famous for. Appearances, however, Chris realized as he crossed the intersection and entered the bar, could be deceiving.

The female couple at one of the low bar tables: Avery and Zoe.

The bartender in his white jacket and thin tie: a Madigan captain.

Two more Madigan captains posing as patrons at the bar.

And around the table in the small dining area at the far end of the space, past the bar, up two steps, and out of view of the big plate-glass windows: Hawes, Holt, and the last person Chris expected to see there, Rose.

The Madigan matriarch looked like the million-plus bucks she was worth, not like she'd been discharged from the hospital earlier this week. She cut a stack of cards with her nimble, ringed fingers and riffled them in a bridge. She glanced up, spotted him, then began doling the cards out into four stacks. The shift in her methodical shuffling drew the twins' attention. Holt gave him a cursory glance, then went about rearranging Lily in her sling. Hawes, unlike his grandmother and brother, tracked Chris's every step as he approached, fiery eyes searing him like they'd done last night. Chris tucked away that memory as fast as it had come, before he embarrassed himself in front of all these people, especially Rose. He figured he was already at the top of her shit list.

Confirmed as she skipped right over his inquiry as to how she was doing, and asked, "Why should I trust you with my family?"

"Because I could have arrested any one of you over the past ten days, and yet, you're sitting here, dealing cards."

Eyes the same blue shade as Hawes's—except as far away from icy hot as humanly possible—pinned him to the spot. "I could also be dead."

"But you're not, because I pushed your car out of the way and put myself in the path of that van."

Risky move, going head to head with her, but Chris didn't think Rose was the type to tolerate, much less appreciate, bullshit. Direct seemed more her style.

She pushed a stack of cards in front of the empty chair to her left. "Sit."

He'd judged correctly, then. "What game are we playing?"

"Hearts," Hawes said from across the table, one corner of his mouth hitched up.

"How's Amelia?" Holt asked as they each passed three cards to the right. "We didn't get to talk to her at the arraignment."

"She's tired, missing you both, and cooperative as a result."

"Did she say who she's working for?" Hawes asked.

Chris shook his head, eyes still on Holt and Lily. "She says she's protecting her family."

"Someone's threatened them," Rose said.

"Maybe someone's threatened all of you."

Holt laid his cards on the table, facedown, and gathered Lily closer to his chest, holding her tight. Hawes grasped his shoulder, squeezing. "We won't let anything happen to Amelia, or to you two."

Rose tossed the two of clubs into the center of the table. "I made a list."

"Can I see it?"

"No." She cut him a withering side-eye. "I wouldn't put it past a few of the names on it to make such threats."

Chris withdrew two sheets of paper from his coat pocket. "Can you tell me if any of these names"—he pushed the residents list to her first, then the photo—"or this man are on it?"

Her eyes flickered to the photo first. "I don't know him." Then she scanned down the residents list, front and back. "None of them either, but Holt, run them against aliases."

"We did that," Chris said. "Came up blank, except for the victim we already knew about."

Holt half coughed, half laughed, while Rose kept her cool tone. "Our resources are more extensive than yours."

Hawes cleared his throat. "We're also seeing if any names crossed paths with Amelia, like we talked about."

Chris was doing the same with the picture and residents list, but if they were going to keep some secrets, so was he.

"Did she confirm the email?" Holt asked.

Chris nodded. "Recruiting Helena was part of the plan, but this is sooner than expected."

"Check the list against Hena too," Hawes said to his brother. "She's impressed someone."

"Not hard to do," Chris said. "She's the scariest of the lot of you."

"And the unlikeliest to turn on her family," Rose said.

She spoke it like it was a given fact, and Chris was surprised neither Hawes nor Holt reacted to or protested the statement. After a moment's consideration, though, Chris had to agree. As far as he knew, as far as his, Izzy's, and Wheeler's research went, Helena didn't have outside influences diverting her loyalty. No children, no partner, no lover. She had her job, but she didn't need it for the money. It was a labor of love, and as long as her clients were taken care of, she could split. Had already been preparing to do so the past week. And while she and Hawes were generally on the same wavelength regarding the organization's targets and direction, Chris imagined Helena's redline was much further out, and a good bit blurrier, than Hawes's. Ruthless, smart, and loyal. Impressive.

"She should remain the point for us," Rose said, drawing Chris back out of his head. "Confirm the meet, but no one is going in alone this time."

Hawes had the good sense to appear chastened. Chris had the good sense to keep the conversation moving while it was going his way. "We're working through the mission parameters on our end. I should have a full workup to share by tomorrow."

"Is Wheeler going to play ball?" Hawes asked.

"He's focused on the explosives now, not on you," Chris told him. "We're all trying to stop the same thing here. The same person. We have been for three years, albeit separately. We can do this together. We're close."

Rose tossed her cards onto the table, ending the half-finished round, and Chris thought he'd lost the hand, lost even more. But then she drained her coffee, stood, and said, "We'll be expecting your call, Agent Perri."

Meeting over, Holt rose beside her, handed Lily to her, and shouldered the diaper bag. They headed out of the restaurant, Avery and Zoe on their heels, while Hawes hung back.

"You handled her well," he said.

Chris met him midway around the table, near the back corner of the room and out of sight of the windows. "She's intimidating as fuck."

Hawes smiled, a bit wistful, a lot somber. "Everyone thought Papa Cal was the scary one."

"She doing okay with that?"

"She did her grieving. She's over it." But Hawes wasn't, judging by the way he averted his gaze. "She was the same way when Mom and Dad died. A wreck for a few days, then completely put back together and in charge."

Stepping closer, Chris lifted a hand and cupped his cheek. "And you? It's only been a week since you lost him too. I'm sorry. I should've asked…"

"When?" Hawes said with a weak laugh. "We haven't had a minute."

That wasn't totally true. "You listened to me as I unloaded this morning about Ro and Izzy. I should have—"

Hawes cut him off with a hand around his wrist. "You needed to tell me that, and I needed to hear it." He turned his face into Chris's palm, nuzzling. Jawbone sharp, stubble prickly, and lips soft as they caressed Chris's skin. "Thank you for trusting me."

Two steps forward and Chris crowded him back against the corner. "I should be thanking you." He pointed at himself. "I'm the fed who lied."

"Good movie title." Hawes loosened his grip and trailed his hand down Chris's forearm, goose bumps lifting in his wake. "And you're not like any fed I've ever known."

"Known a few, have you?"

He shrugged one shoulder, and the opposite corner of his mouth hitched up, the hint of a smirk chasing away the melancholy. The next instant, Chris was wrenched forward by the arm, spun, and shoved front first into the corner. Hawes's heat slammed into his back and wafted over his ear, lips and breath tickling there. "You're my favorite."

Chris's stomach flipped, and his dick hardened. "Good to know, and fuck them."

Hawes laughed and nipped his nape. "Tomorrow, Agent Perri."

"Tomorrow," Chris repeated to Hawes's backside as the king, head held high, strode out of the restaurant and into the night.

Chris waited long enough for his erection to subside, then paid the table's bill, crossed the street, and turned down the alley where he'd parked the Hog. And found he wasn't alone. Hawes stood leaning against the wall across from the bike, knee bent, one foot propped on the cinder blocks. Fog crept around the ankle of his other leg, around the slits of his suit coat, and overhead in the faint halo of light cast by the street lamps at either end of the alley.

In the blue eyes that swiveled Chris's direction.

Chris took a mental picture, the essence of Hawes Madigan captured in a single shot. Like the fog he loved so much, Hawes was a creature of shadow and light, playing in the corners, at the edges, until the wispy, indefinable mist slunk in all around and was too overpowering to see your way out of. You could fear it, fear the uncertainty, or let go and accept it. In this city, there was no escaping it. So you grew to love it. Like Hawes had the fog, like Chris had the man.

Fuck, he'd totally fallen for the mark.

Priorities shifted with each step Chris took toward Hawes. Keeping this man alive rocketed even higher up the ladder. Finding Isabella's killer was paramount. Securing the explosives and Hawes's empire likewise near the top. But it wasn't only because Chris agreed that less death was a good thing or because he was on board with the way Hawes ran things. Chris wanted—needed—Hawes to be alive at the end of all this. Hawes could take care of himself, he'd proven that time and again, but after almost watching him die yesterday, feeling like the bottom had dropped out of his world for a third time, he couldn't handle that reality coming to pass.

Not when an alternate reality was making itself known. His head wasn't totally on board yet, unsure how to make their differing approaches to justice work, but his heart had tasted home again and was loath to part with it. Or with the man who'd stoked that feeling to life.

"Are you on board with this plan?" Chris said as he approached.

"Did you hear me object?"

"I didn't hear you say much of anything." Chris rested carefully back against the bike. An exercise in balance, and in restraint, every muscle in his body screaming to press along Hawes's, to claim another taste of home, but he needed to make his point. Needed to be sure. "I need to know you're on the same page. That we're in this together."

Hawes leaned his head back and stared at the sky. "It would be a tactical error, keeping you out of the loop again."

"Fuck the tactical reasons." The frustrated bark in Chris's voice jerked Hawes's gaze back to him. "I'm talking about keeping you alive. Because yesterday can't happen again."

"You know what I am. I know what you are. Let's not be naive. Death is always a risk."

Chris hung his head, curled one hand around a handlebar, and the other around the leather seat, and inhaled deeply.

"I don't want to lose you either," Hawes whispered from across the alley, voice as tortured as Chris's insides. Full of the same storm of emotions Chris was fighting, brought on by realities that couldn't be denied. Acknowledged, then, but so too had been what was at stake for both of them.

Fuck restraint. Chris pushed off the bike and closed the distance between them. He bent his head and swirled his tongue in the deep groove between Hawes's neck and shoulder. "Did those other feds know how you like to be kissed, right here?"

Hawes whimpered and threaded a hand through Chris's hair, holding him there. Chris enjoyed the tugging hold while he nipped at Hawes's collarbone, then soothed the freckled skin with his tongue. But as he trailed a line of kisses to Hawes's ear, he grasped Hawes's wrist, withdrew his hand from his hair, and pinned his arm to the wall. "Did they know how you like to let go?" He rolled his hips, and Hawes rocked back.

"They didn't know me like this. No one has." He leaned in for a kiss, and Chris dodged. "Dante, please."

Chris pressed against him, a rolling wave of need cresting from thighs, to groin, to chest, to the breath across Hawes's cheek and the hand tangled with his. And at each point of contact, Hawes rolled back with the same need. "Did they know what it's like to have all this writhing under them?" He kissed down Hawes's cheekbone and snaked a hand between them to cup Hawes through his slacks. "What a fucking gift all this is?"

A tremble wracked Hawes's body, and he froze. Chris leaned back far enough to see his face, afraid he'd said or done something wrong. But it wasn't anger or confusion staring back at him. Instead, Hawes's eyes were wide and full of chilly sorrow. "I'm no one's gift. A curse maybe…"

"Wrong." Chris kissed him hard, blasting heat to chip away at that damnable ice. "And even if you were a curse, I'd have no interest in breaking it."

"You're just going to break me."

"Good, then we'll be even."

Hawes laughed, deep and rumbly, breaking the tension, and breaking any hope Chris had of holding back. He crushed his mouth against Hawes's, and from there it was a race to see who could break the other faster. Pants ripped open, hands dove into boxers, fists wrapped around cocks, stroking each other in the darkness, the cool fog curling around them, hiding them in their own little world of heat and desperation.

It was reckless, sharing this here in a public alley, doing this at all, for both of them, but putting on the brakes was no longer an option. And when Hawes took both of them in hand, exerting control, Chris scrabbled at the wall on either side of Hawes's head, struggling to hold himself up against the onslaught of pleasure. Gasping between frantic, hungry kisses, he thrust into Hawes's fist, against his long, hard cock, foot on the gas, speeding them toward orgasm.

When they came together, Chris's hand covering Hawes's, clasped around their cocks, the both of them rutting and spilling over their tangled fingers, "Even" was on Hawes's lips, and a prayer was on Chris's, a fervent wish that this spell never be broken.

FOURTEEN

Chris's head was still spinning the next morning from the surreal meeting with the Madigans—and the surreal after-encounter with Hawes in the alley. So much so that he would've fucked up Mia's omelet if not for Marco snatching the bag of chopped ham out of his hand.

"She's a vegetarian this week, remember?" his nephew said.

"Good catch, kid." He reclaimed the bag and dumped the remaining meat in the other skillet, making Marco a double-stuffed Denver.

Marco laughed. "Thinking you need coffee as much as I do." He reached for the pot, and Gloria swooped in, batting his hand down.

"The answer is no," she said.

"Ang is just going to stop and get us venti iced lattes on the way to Marco's day camp," Mia said from the table, where she sat with an e-reader propped in front of her. "Her favorite coffee shop is in that neighborhood."

"But I didn't serve it to you," Gloria said. "Your mom's rules."

Marco made a Vanna White worthy sweep of the room with his eyes and arms. "I don't see Mom, do you?"

Chris bumped his hip. "Go sit down, Plato. Not the time to argue."

Mia rolled her eyes. "He has so lived up to that nickname."

Laughter broke the tension, but not Chris's concern, which had been piqued by Marco's throwaway comment. Where was Celia?

He slid each omelet out of its skillet and onto a plate and carried them over to the table, where he slipped a ten to each of the kids. Marco gave him a fist bump, Mia a smile. He'd take that and the way they happily dug into their food.

He returned to the cutting boards and utensils in the sink and his mother's knowing grin. "I saw that."

"Like Mia said, they're gonna get it anyway. Angelica shouldn't have to foot the bill. And she made me a box of mistletoe cannoli."

"And the truth comes out." Gloria drained her first cup, then refilled it and one for him too. He finished filling the sink with soap and water, then wiped his hands off and accepted the offered brew. She added, "Thanks for helping out this morning."

He lowered his voice so the kids wouldn't hear him. "You said your gout was acting up, but you're moving around just fine, so why am I really here?" She glanced over her shoulder at the kids, confirming Chris's suspicion. "Where's Celia?"

Before she could answer, a car horn blew outside, and his niblings clicked into fast-forward, shoving last bites into their mouths and stuffing their scattered daily detritus into bookbags.

"Dishes in the sink," Gloria said, and they scurried over to drop their plates in the soapy water.

Marco gave them both a hug. Mia gave Gloria's cheek a kiss and Chris a wave of her e-reader, and then they were gone, the slam of doors and the squeal of Angelica's tires outside making Chris laugh. Of all the Perris, his cousin had the heaviest foot and the speeding tickets to prove it.

Chris returned to the sink and dipped his hands beneath the suds. "You didn't answer my question," he said to his mom as he scrubbed dishes. "Where's Celia?"

"Right here. And I'm fine."

He turned his head the opposite direction, toward his sister's voice, and thanked the saints that his hands—no, his fists—were hidden under the water. His sister was clearly not fine. Her slight frame drowned in the folds of their dad's old flannel robe, but Chris supposed it gave her some comfort. Some protection against the reality of her black eye, busted lip, and hobbled gait as she slowly crossed the living room toward them.

Mia's worry from the other night had come to pass.

"I'm gonna fucking kill him." So much for keeping his anger in check.

"Don't," she said, gingerly lowering herself into the chair Mia had vacated. "He's not worth it. I'd rather you help me get a restraining order."

About fucking time. "Done." He grabbed the last dish, rinsed it off, and set it in the rack to drip dry. "I know a lawyer. It's not what she does, but she knows everyone. She'll make it happen." He figured this was right up Helena's alley, in more ways than one. And Kane would be more than happy to enforce said order. "He won't come near you again, Cee."

Gloria set a steaming mug in front of her, then claimed the chair beside her. "And you won't go back to him either."

Celia looked away from them, swallowing hard. With a clear view of her blackened eye, of the finger bruises on her neck that her hair had hidden, Chris had to wrap a towel around his fists to keep from punching through the wall. "Where is he? So we'll know where to serve him."

Celia laughed, tired and bitter. "So you can go beat him up? No, not that I have any idea where he went...after..." She gestured at her face, then cinched the robe tighter around herself.

Fuck, the last thing she needed right now was him in rage mode too. He unwound the cloth, took a deep breath, and sat in the chair across from them. "I know this is tough—"

"What do you know about this?" Celia snapped. Her dark eyes sparked to match, but not with anger, with hurt and regret. "You're never here."

Chris raised his hands, palms out. "You're right. I have been gone too much, but I'm hoping to change that." Aside from the momentary panic when he'd thought Hawes was dead, his hope and commitment to stay had only solidified over the past week and a half. He wanted—needed—to stay. For whatever this thing was with Hawes and for his family.

But his sister didn't look happy about that declaration. She cast her gaze aside again and swallowed hard.

"You don't want me here?" Chris said.

"Of course I want you here."

"Then what is it?"

She righted her gaze, and there were tears in her dark eyes, one escaping and racing down her bruised cheek. "She looked so much like you." Her voice wobbled—"It's my fault"—and broke, Celia with it, as she covered her face and cried into her hands.

Chris's heart broke too, for all that they'd lost, and for the weight of it that Celia had been carrying, because he'd run from it, hadn't been around to help her shoulder the load, to tell her she didn't need to shoulder it at all. This was the damage he'd done.

He rose, circled the table, and knelt by his sister's side. "Fuck, Cee, I'm sorry," he said, and when she wouldn't give him her eyes, he lightly grasped her chin and rotated her gaze to him. "You are the last person I blame for what happened to Ro. If you hadn't been driving, we would have lost you and Mia too." He cupped her unbruised cheek. "Please stop blaming yourself."

She hid her face in his hand. "I keep replaying that day. If I'd done something different, if I'd not taken that shortcut…"

"Stop." He rose and gently pulled her into a hug. "It's been ten years, Cee. Stop punishing yourself. Stop letting him punish you." Because that's what she'd been doing. Taking the hits because she thought she deserved them. He held her as tightly as her injuries would allow. "Your whole life has been stuck there, honey. Ro wouldn't want that."

The damn broke, her sobs coming loud and ragged, and the tension finally, finally, flowed from her body. Chris held his sister like he should have more often the past decade, not the awkward hugs of strangers, but of two people who'd been best friends growing up, who'd always had each other's backs.

Gloria scooted closer, rubbing her daughter's back. "Everything changed that day. We lost Ro, but we also lost you."

Celia drew back, wiping the tears from under her eyes and the wetness from under Chris's eyes as well. "We lost you too that day," she said to him. "Ro wouldn't want that either."

Everything had changed ten years ago. He'd lost the center of his world, been set adrift, and almost turned the lights out on himself. But Izzy had found him and changed the course of his life. And he'd been punishing himself ever since. Jumping from one undercover assignment to another, pretending to be someone he wasn't, so he could block out all he'd lost. It had worked when he'd needed it to, but now? Being back here with his family, being with Hawes, a little of the old Christopher and a little of the new Dante were blending together—someone who was the same but not, the reality of himself now, and he was looking for a port to come home to, but the fog made it hard to navigate. Fog from all the years spent thinking himself weak in that moment of darkness, from the mistakes he'd made. Because he also felt responsible for not being there then, and now. And the past three years, he'd thrown himself into the hunt for Izzy's killer. Another distraction, another act of retribution and self-blame.

Retribution. Self-blame.

Chris froze, the words echoing in his head, shifting his

frame of reference as puzzle pieces of a different sort fell into place.

Everything changed that night.

The night of Isabella's death.

Because Hawes felt responsible.

Or because he was responsible?

Chris was glad he'd taken the Hog to his mom's place. It had made navigating back home easier. Faster. Less time for him to jump to conclusions without first reexamining the evidence from the night of Izzy's death. Reconsidering that night that had changed everything from a different perspective. Not from his own, as an outside investigator. Not from his partner's, as the victim. From Hawes's. As the what?

Just like Chris's life had changed the day Ro had died, Hawes's life, and the trajectory of his organization, had changed the night Isabella died. Chris had witnessed those changes in action, had counted on them in revealing certain information to Hawes, and was working with Hawes to protect them from those who wanted to go back to the old ways.

Under Hawes's regime, targets had to be vetted and collateral damage eliminated. Lofty morals for an assassin descended from parents who, by all accounts, were efficient killing machines, much like Helena. From a grandmother who wielded words like Holt did his keystrokes. And a grandfather who'd built an empire on fear, much like the Prince of Killers moniker Hawes hated but stoked when needed.

A new regime that had come into being after Izzy's death.

Why? Izzy asked in Chris's head. *What changed for him that night?*

Why did Hawes, like Celia, feel responsible? He wasn't exactly punishing himself like Chris's sister, but he'd changed his whole life as a result of that night.

Chris paced the study as he talked it out with his partner. "Because his family was threatened. Infiltrated by the ATF. He didn't want it to happen again."

Except that wasn't right. Genuine surprise and betrayal had flashed across Hawes's face when Chris had revealed his and Izzy's true identities. He hadn't known last week, much less three years ago, that his organization had been so deeply infiltrated by the ATF. That wasn't the reason.

What's the other side of that coin?

"He thought you were an innocent." He turned on his heel to face the collage of crime scene photos and notes. Izzy's and Zander Rowe's sheet-covered bodies on the rain-slicked street. The reflection of blue and red lights, evidence markers, and two pistols. "One of his employees, a secretary, who was trying to defend herself, killed by one of his lieutenants." Hawes cared about the legit organization as much as the illegal one. He'd take it personally, bear the brunt of the responsibility, if one of those employees was unwittingly caught in the crossfire.

What crossfire?

It sure as fuck hadn't been a domestic disturbance. While evidence at the scene pointed to that easily enough—Izzy's mangled wrists, the bruises on her face—none of Izzy's notes indicated Rowe had been abusive. And none of the Madigan siblings would have put up with that sort of behavior had they gotten so much as a whiff of it.

Fuck, how did he make the pieces of this puzzle fit? What was he missing? It was all there. He just had to figure out what tied it all together.

Hands on his head, he rotated slowly around the room, halting in front of the current investigation notes.

The explosives.

"That was your mission. You found something. Is that why Rowe killed you?"

They were connected to all this, and Hawes was doing everything he could to get the organization out of that business. Too much of a risk, too high a cost, he'd said last week. The definition of collateral damage.

No collateral damage.

"That's what you were." Not a mole, not caught up in a domestic disturbance. No, as far as Hawes knew, she'd been Rowe's girlfriend, and that night, she'd been in the wrong place, at the wrong time. "Unacceptable collateral damage."

Chris rushed the desk full of notes and began pulling sheets of paper and tacking them to the wall in a separate collage. Repositioned crime scene photos to go with them. The things that never quite added up. A Madigan company sedan at the scene, but no hair or fiber from Izzy or Rowe inside it. Tire tracks and skid marks that didn't match the sedan. That were more likely a van or truck. Like the van loaded with explosives that had tried to kill Hawes after Papa Cal's funeral. He snatched the bank record showing Amelia's deposit to Zander Rowe and added it to the story.

"Rowe was a traitor. Diverting a van of explosives. And you found out." The last report she'd filed—the night she'd died—was that someone else was trying to buy the explosives. She'd found out, and the neo-Nazi who died Tuesday was at the top of her suspects list.

No, the neo-Nazi who was killed. *By…*

"Hawes. He found out too."

Which would be unacceptable to the then prince. The potential for collateral damage—to his family, their empire, and his city—would be too high.

What'd he do, Dante?

Ice crept through his veins as the jagged puzzle pieces began to match up, began to fit into a picture that was still blurry, but which some inherent part of him knew he didn't want to see. Not the picture of home he'd been putting together. A nightmare instead, like the one Hawes suffered —*replayed*—nightly.

"He intercepted the van."

Not just ice anymore. A whole mountain of snow buried him in an avalanche as actions and words from the past week played through his mind.

Hawes's revulsion at the gun Chris had shoved in his hand. *"They kill too fast,"* Hawes had said. *"Without thought. It's too easy to make the wrong call."* In every fight, the assassin had used a different weapon—his body, a garrote, his words. Until Friday morning, when he'd picked up Chris's gun, and Helena had been shocked and terrified.

Why?

Chris guessed the terrible truth. "Because he hadn't touched one in three years."

Then he hunted for the evidence to disprove what he didn't want to believe. Rifling back through Izzy's files, he searched for pictures of Hawes from before Izzy's death.

A photo of him at MCS, dressed in one of his fitted suits, a visible bulge under his left arm.

On the yacht, a bump on his right hip under the hem of his sweater.

He used to carry.

Until he'd made the wrong call.

He flipped to the next picture in the file.

Hawes, in a fog-filled alley, a gun pointed at a man on his knees.

A Colt 1911.

The same type of gun on the ground next to Zander Rowe's body. The gun that had fired the bullet that killed Izzy. A gun that wasn't registered to Zander Rowe. That they'd never been able to trace. They'd thought it had been Rowe's, obtained illegally.

Whose was it, Dante?

Bile surged up Chris's throat, and he braced his hands on the wall, on either side of the ad hoc story he'd constructed. Of the assembled puzzle in front of him, the nightmare crystal fucking clear.

No indiscriminate killing. The last of Hawes's rules. Something a gun tended to do. The weapon Hawes wouldn't use. The rule and aversion the very opposite of the title that had been bestowed on him.

The Prince of Killers.

Why does he hate it so much?

"Because he thinks he killed his parents." Hawes had told him that story. How he'd been the one to give the order to pull the plug and take his parents off life support. But that wasn't the only reason. Those weren't the only deaths Hawes regretted. There was another one staring Chris right in the face. A truth that kept Hawes up at night, that he and his siblings had tiptoed around in conversation, that Hawes had apologized for the other night, only Chris hadn't understood then.

He understood now. His gut burned, and his chest ached, ripped apart by another loss—his hope for a future, a *home*, bleeding out on the hardwood floor. Like Izzy had bled out that night in the street, murdered by the same man Chris had fallen for.

Who else did he kill, Dante?

Pushing past the pain, he spoke the truth that had eluded him for three long years. "You."

FIFTEEN

Chris ignored the vibrating phone in his pocket, same as he'd ignored the other umpteen calls today while he'd been adjusting his frame of reference. Rearranging the evidence into a picture that was indisputable. Replaying every interaction he'd had with Hawes Madigan.

Betrayal stung hot and deep. Fucking karma.

Until this morning, Chris had been sincere in his aim to help Hawes hold on to power. The direction Hawes and his siblings were taking the organization, the rules they followed, did result in less death. Only the worst criminals, those who'd escaped the justice Chris and the law doled out, met their end. As much as Chris wanted to believe the rule of law was enough, he wasn't a total fool.

But knowing the why now, knowing that Hawes had been undercutting Chris's primary mission at every turn, knowing that Isabella's killer had been staring him right in the face, kissing him, writhing under him, had sent Chris gagging over the toilet more than once today.

Disgust and damnable desire still churned in his gut,

but anger fueled his footsteps up the stairs, two at a time, to Kane's office. He banged open the stairwell door, glimpsed the directional signage, and diverted. He wanted to check something else first. Another thing that didn't line up about that night.

He found the IT department, and Jax's platinum Mohawk was like a beacon, drawing him to their workstation. They spotted him several desks away and reared back in their chair. Chris slowed his gait and reined in his glare. He needed their help, but he was taking a gamble. Jax had only started at SFPD last year. He didn't think they would have been involved three years ago, but they were one of Holt's kids. There was no way to know for sure what they might have done off-book before joining the force. If nothing else, Chris was sure they would report this encounter.

"Agent Perri," they greeted cautiously. "What's going on?"

He pulled a flash drive from his jacket pocket. "Cue that up."

They gave him the same skeptical raised brow Holt had when Chris had earlier presented him with a flash drive. "It's SFPD's own footage, from a previous crime scene."

"If this has a—"

"No virus. I wouldn't know how anyway."

They still ran a virus check after inserting the device and before clicking any of its contents. That done, Jax opened the video footage and pressed Play.

And nothing. As frustratingly boring as it had always been. Just a recording of the rain-slick street that cut off before Isabella and Rowe ever appeared.

"I don't get it," Jax said.

"According to the police report, the traffic cam that captured this intersection cycled off two minutes before a double homicide occurred here." He tapped the screen. "Can you tell if that's the case?"

"It is," they answered immediately. "But it's been looped before that."

"Excuse me?"

"Right before the cutoff. It's a loop feed. A very well-executed one, but it's a loop. I'm color blind." They pointed to a Golden State Warriors flag hanging over a shop door in the far-right corner of the screen. "That flag is royal blue and yellow to you. To me, it's navy and white, as in bright white, which really shows in the dark." Their fingers raced across the keyboard, and a second later, the picture was in monochrome "Take out the color saturation, and the details pop for you too." Indeed, Chris noticed it more clearly now. "You see it move?"

He nodded. "With the wind."

"The exact same way?" They rewound the footage, slowed it down, and sure enough, it was an exact replica. More like a blip than a nudge from the breeze. "And look at the reflection in the puddle." Of the neon red CLOSED sign in a storefront window, with a news ticker below, displaying the same line of text.

"Fuck." But it was still cut off before the incident. What had they hidden in those few seconds? The van coming into the scene? Someone else—Hawes—arriving there too? "Can you recover the altered footage?"

They shook their head. "Past the three-year archive mark. But I'm the best here at finding hidden code." Fingers flew again. "It's got to be buried here somewhere." Another two minutes in which Chris tried not to lose what little was left of his shit, and then they stopped typing abruptly.

Chris glanced at the screen, at the string of numbers that didn't mean a thing to him but clearly translated for Jax. "What is it?"

"Nothing. There's nothing here."

Chris grabbed the arm of their chair and spun them around to face him. "You're doing good work here. You've come a long way from the shelter. Don't risk that."

"I can't get the footage."

"But you know who made the change." He glanced at the screen. "Your mentor, Holt, I'm guessing?"

"Not exactly." They tapped a nail against the armrest, reticent to say more.

Which was more than enough for Chris. If it wasn't Holt, there was only one other person Jax would protect with their silence. And as luck would have it, he worked in this very same building.

Kane stood behind his desk, waiting at military attention. Legs spread, arms crossed over his chest, he didn't blink, didn't flinch, when Chris charged into his office and slammed the door behind him.

"What happened the night Isabella died?" Chris demanded.

"That was before I was chief."

"But you were here, on the force, weren't you?"

"I'd come on about eighteen months before."

Wasn't that convenient? The Madigans' pet cop showed up shortly after Hawes's ascension. Had they always planned it that way? Probably. Chris didn't think it was by chance.

He tossed the flash drive onto the desk. "You altered the surveillance footage from the night Izzy died."

Kane paled and dug his fingers into his biceps, but he didn't say a word to confirm or deny.

Chris stepped forward, thighs butting the edge of the desk in front of him. "You helped them cover it up."

"I don't know what you're talking about."

Chris scoffed. "Did you know they left a clue in the system?"

"There's no evidence—"

"Jax is a better hacker than you or Holt think."

Kane's brows dipped into a *V*, but he kept his lips pressed together, silent.

"Don't have your orders yet, do you?"

The chief of police, the man charged with upholding the law in San Francisco, took his cue not from the law, but from an organization of assassins. Twelve hours ago, Chris thought maybe that worked. That the delicate balance was needed. Not anymore. And judging by his locked-down, cold demeanor, Kane wasn't looking at Chris as an ally anymore either. In front of him stood Agent Perri, the man who could blow apart his entire house of cards. Given what was at stake, and Kane's military training, this exercise was futile. He wasn't going to crack.

"I need to talk to Amelia," Chris said.

"She's already been transferred out."

Of course she had. Growling, Chris flung out an arm and whacked the candy bowl off the desk. The carpet prevented it from shattering, but caramel candies went flying, pinging off the walls and floor. "Then *you're* going to give me some fucking answers, or I'll—"

"You'll what?"

Chris whipped around to the woman who had the most impeccable timing in the world, and a knife in her hand, the razor-sharp tip now pressing into the tender spot beneath his last rib. "Haven't we been here before, Mr. Hair? Did you not learn your lesson about making threats?"

"Of course you're here."

Helena shrugged and pressed a measure harder with the knife, only a flick of her wrist away from drawing blood, or worse. "What was that threat you were about to make?"

Well, he'd needed to talk to her anyway. The day had gone sideways, and he'd lost sight of another of his priorities. Here was a chance to fix that at least. "Two things," he said to her. "One, I need a good family lawyer."

Helena tilted her head, eyes narrowed. "You?"

"My sister. Husband beat her up. Needs a TRO and a divorce."

No hesitation, no flinch. "Done."

"Two, did Hawes kill Isabella?"

That made her flinch, and it was as good a confirmation as any.

Fuck.

This whole time, his partner's killer had been right there in front of him, under him, in his arms, in his fucking bed. He stumbled back against the desk's edge and hung his head. "And I thought *I* was fooling *you all.*"

They'd fooled Kane too, judging by the man's muttered curse.

"You didn't know?" Chris asked over his shoulder.

Kane collapsed into his chair and covered his face with

his hands. More than enough betrayal to go around it seemed.

"Hawes was fooled too," Helena said, drawing Chris's attention back to her. She'd stepped back and stashed the knife God only knew where. "He thought she was an accomplice, and then he thought she was an innocent. It's torn him up every day for the past three years, and then you show up and hammer that nail even harder. But she was neither of those things, was she? She was an agent, she knew what she was getting into, she knew the risks. Same as you. He was set up, just like the rest of us."

"He fucking shot her, and all week, he—*all of you*—let me think it was someone else."

"It *was* someone else," Kane said, and Chris whipped back around, glaring. "Do you remember what Amelia said? Whoever she's working for knew who you were before you got here. I'm guessing they knew who your partner was too. Helena's right. Hawes may have pulled the trigger, but someone put him and your partner there."

"Right now, that someone else isn't my fucking problem." He pushed off the desk and used his full height to loom over Helena. "Where is he?"

"Not a chance, Mr. Hair."

He shoved past her toward the door. "You better hope you find him before I do."

SIXTEEN

Helena had found Hawes first, or at a minimum, delivered a warning to him, because wherever Chris looked, Hawes wasn't there. The cold storage facility on the docks, the warehouse in South City, the company yacht. The South Beach condo, the family fort in Pac Heights, the ballpark. Chris had flashed his badge to get in and scouted the entire club-level concourse. Like a ghost, Hawes had vanished. Chris didn't think he'd left town, not with so much uncertainty hanging over his family and his organization. And he wouldn't leave Helena unguarded tomorrow, but he was apparently playing Casper until he had to show himself.

Probably better that way. Chris had a fucking op to prepare for, one that depended on the Madigans' cooperation, one that could save countless lives, but all Chris could focus on was the life that had been lost. And the man who'd stolen it. The man who'd stolen something else from Chris that left his chest aching, his gut twisted, and his entire being hollowed out and drifting, no longer at home in the fog. Suffocating under the weight of it.

Frustrated and empty-handed, Chris was in a mood that matched the night sky by the time he returned to his condo. Home. Didn't much feel like it anymore, just when it had recently begun to for the first time in a decade. Trudging up the steps, Chris curled and flexed his fingers, itching to tear the place apart. To tear anything apart.

He opened the front door and got his wish in the form of a six-foot-two, blue-eyed, suited assassin standing calmly by his kitchen island.

With a gun in his hand.

Chris had misjudged him once again. Hawes hadn't been playing Casper at all. He'd come directly here to face the truth. What was it he'd said? He was done with this shit. Apparently so. Hawes squared his shoulders and lifted the arm holding the gun. Chris closed his hand around the grip of the backup weapon in his holster, but then released it when Hawes placed his—no, Chris's gun, from Friday—on the island next to a bottle of Crown Royal Rye, the same they'd shared at Hawes's condo. "I didn't mean to leave you defenseless."

Defenseless. Apt description. Sure, he had a gun within reach, but the absence of truth was far more deadly. Chris slammed the door shut, tossed his jacket in a corner, and stalked across the space between them. No more lies. "Why did everything change that night?"

Defiant, resigned eyes stared back at him, a winter storm swirling in their depths. "Because I shot Isabelle Costa."

Chris grabbed him by the jacket lapels, spun, and slammed him against the wall between the study and bedroom. "You killed her? Not Rowe?"

Despite the manhandling, Hawes didn't fight back and gave no sign of distress. "I did," he answered flatly.

Cold, untouchable. Now Chris got it. And it only amped up his anger, made it burn hotter. "You knew why I was here, what I was looking for, and you let the past week and a half slip by without a word."

"You were using me. I was using you."

Chris flattened his hands on Hawes's chest and pushed, slamming him against the wall again. "We're way past that, and you fucking know it."

"I think the same person behind the coup was behind that night."

Anger erupted at the deflection, at Hawes's ability to keep that cool, flat tone when Chris's world was coming apart at the seams. "You pulled the fucking trigger! Maybe you are a fucking curse."

Finally, a reaction. Hawes whipped his head to the side as if he'd been slapped. He stared out the back windows, Adam's apple bobbing erratically.

Chris cupped the side of his face, far from gentle, a thumb wedged under his chin, his fingers splayed over his cheek, the grip secure. "And after what I told you the other morning, about Ro, about how Izzy saved me, you still didn't tell me the truth. I trusted you. I lo—" Hawes tried to jerk free, and the pressure that exerted on Chris's hold tripped up his words before he uttered the last thing either of them needed. "Fuck!"

Hawes's response came out a hoarse whisper. "I still don't know who set her up to die."

Chris forced his face back around. "Does it matter? You pulled the trigger. You killed her."

Hawes lowered his eyes, long lashes brushing his pale cheeks. "I'm so sorry, Dant—"

"Don't! You don't get to use that name anymore." Not now that the spell was well and truly broken. He pressed his fingertips into the hollow of Hawes's cheek, demanding his gaze again. "It meant I mattered to someone again, to her. And she mattered too."

"She did."

Cold, hard metal pressed against Chris's stomach. He glanced down, then back up in surprise. In his anger, in the flurry of earlier movement, he hadn't noticed Hawes snatch the gun off the island, hadn't realized he'd been at Hawes's mercy this entire time. And now Hawes was at his, Hawes shoving the gun at Chris butt-first, barrel pointing at his own gut.

"She did matter," Hawes said, voice rough, his icy exterior shattering with each word. "And I'm willing to lose everything for her now. I pulled the trigger. I relive that night over and over. I did it, yes, but I want to know who put me and her in that position, who brought you to my doorstep three years later, who knew you'd be my weakness."

He pressed the gun harder into Chris's abs, waiting for him to take hold of it, and only continuing once he had. "I want to know the whole truth, and so do you. More than that, I want to stop it from ever happening again, and I can't do that alone. I went into this using you, but you're right—we flew way past that, and now I need you. Help me stop this, and then I'll turn myself over to you, on or off the books."

Chris moved the gun out from between them and eased

his grip on Hawes's face, but he didn't step back, held there by truth and lies and all the gray space between them. "After the strike tomorrow."

Hawes nodded. "We shut this down, and then I'm yours."

SEVENTEEN

Chris found Wheeler in the war room, as expected. Tie gone, sleeves rolled up, he was shuffling through surveillance photos and street maps with one hand and tapping out a staccato rhythm with the pen in his other. "You've been trying to reach me," Chris said, making his presence known.

Wheeler's head shot up, gaze surprised, then furious. "For an entire fucking day." His temper quelled, though, at whatever he saw on Chris's face. He dialed it down from a ten to a tolerable five. "You haven't been answering my calls and you've been ignoring my voice mails."

"One, learn to text. Two, I was sorting some stuff out, which we'll get to in a minute." He lowered himself into the chair across the table. "But first, is this the tactical plan for tomorrow?"

"Yeah, based on our work yesterday."

Chris nodded. "Okay, give me the rundown."

Wheeler walked him through it, step-by-step—the pick-up, the approach, the convergence, the attack, and the seizure. Assuming all went according to plan. He had contingencies mapped out, multiple means of transport ready, and surveillance points and tactical check-ins every step of the way. He'd done good work, had coordinated with SFPD seamlessly, and all systems were a go for the operation. Chris intended to follow ninety-nine percent of the plan. He didn't think Wheeler would mind the one percent change.

"That's not exactly how the op is going to go down," he said.

Fury returned as Wheeler shot to his feet. "I'm sorry, *what*?" He expected Chris to override him, to scrap the tactical plan he'd lost God only knew how many hours of sleep over.

"Hear me out," Chris said. "I want the same thing you do."

"To secure the explosives."

"And to bring down the Madigans."

After the confrontation with Hawes, he'd walked the park for an hour, debating Hawes's offer. *I'm yours.* To kill, to fuck, to arrest, to walk away from.

To keep.

That last option had driven him here. He couldn't keep Hawes and get justice for Izzy. They were incompatible. Hawes had killed Izzy. Chris had to bring the ATF in on this because it was what she deserved, and because the temptation to do otherwise was a siren song he didn't know if he could resist, even through a hurricane of betrayal.

Brown eyes wide, Wheeler barely managed to aim his ass into his chair as he fell back into it. "Since when?"

"Since I found out who killed my partner."

"What did you find out?"

"That it wasn't a domestic disturbance, that the Madigans covered it up, and that the person who pulled the trigger isn't the only one responsible." He wasn't willing to turn over all his cards—Chris would only completely trust himself now—but Wheeler could help win the hand. "I want all of them, and the explosives are the common thread."

"I may have a lead on that." Wheeler bounded out of his chair, no longer unsure, and darted for the stack of files at the other end of the conference table. He dug out a manila folder, and from it, photos of their mystery man from the auction site. "He's not a building resident, but I used the surveillance time stamp and the building access logs to see which units were pinged for entry at the time he arrived. There were two, and when I searched each of those residents' social media feeds, I found this." He handed Chris a second photo, a screenshot of an Instagram feed.

This was why you wanted Scotty Wheeler on your cases. Never met a haystack he didn't like. "Karen Alexander," he said. "Unit 501."

Chris examined the photo.

The twenty-something blonde, dressed for a day of sailing, stood on the deck of a boat, the Bay Bridge in the background, their mystery man at her side. Chris read the caption, dated the morning of the op: *Thanks for the tug, GB. Dinner on me tonight?*

"Gilbert Baker," Wheeler said, beating Chris to the question. "He runs a tug and"—he curled his fingers in air quotes—"salvage operation out of China Basin."

"And by salvage you mean smuggler."

"Never charged officially."

"Of course not. Wouldn't be in business long if he had."

Chris worked through this new development. "He's not high-level enough to be competition for the Madigans, but if you were in the market for explosives and needed to move them…"

"He would be your guy." A stack of stapled papers—a list—appeared under his nose. "The people he does business with."

Chris whistled low. It wasn't a short list, and many of the names—legitimate and otherwise—were recognizable, including one from Izzy's files. "Carl Reeves is on this list."

Reeves's front company, a shipping business, had contracts with MCS. Izzy had suspected there was more to it than supplying freezer units for his shipping vessels but had never gotten the evidence she needed to officially pursue the lead. She'd sniffed around, though. If Reeves had gotten wind of that, of Izzy, if he'd dug into those investigating him, maybe he'd learned who Izzy really was. Who Chris was. If they were looking for a player with the juice to move everyone around the board, Reeves fit the bill. And a hostile takeover of the Madigans would fit the bill too. Vertical integration for his legit business. Trained assassins and a stockpile of explosives to protect his other enterprise. A force on land and on sea.

Wheeler lowered himself back into the chair across from Chris. "I'm guessing Karen's boat didn't just happen to have engine failure that day."

"Good guess."

Reeves would have seen the Madigans auction notice on the dark web and been looking for a way in, a way to set the trap. Gilbert secured entry and likely smuggled those explosives into the building.

"His contracts with the Madigans began to dwindle five

years ago, then were completely terminated at the three-year mark."

"Because Hawes didn't want anything to do with him."

"Or because Reeves knew they'd been infiltrated. It's all tied together," Wheeler said with a nod. "I believe you."

And now Reeves was reaching out to Helena. Overthrowing the man who'd ruined his plan and installing a new queen for his empire. Chris had other ideas. "Check his connections to all the siblings and to Rose." The matriarch wasn't just sitting by. She had effectively run that meeting at the Buena Vista. Was she also running something on the side? Was she unhappy with the more restrained direction her grandkids were taking the company? "Let's be ready so when we catch him, all of them, in our trap, we can take them down."

Wheeler's grin was just shy of feral. "The King Slayer came to play."

Chris forced himself not to cringe, the instinct automatic. But the King Slayer was who he needed to be right now, to take down the man who wanted to be king and to get justice against the king who'd killed his partner. The King Slayer could silence the sirens, forget the picture of home they sang of.

"I'm assuming you can adjust the strike plan?" he said to Wheeler. "We secure the explosives, then we secure the targets. All of them."

"I need a couple more agents. Two, maybe three."

"Vet them." Chris did cringe then, reminded of Amelia's jab. He did sound like Hawes, but in this instance, their op depended on it. They couldn't have any leaks. "If they're clear, bring them in."

"Kane?" Wheeler asked.

Chris shook his head. "Compromised." Then almost laughed out loud at the pot-kettle irony of labeling Kane compromised when he'd been the one jerking Hawes off in an alley last night. But it wasn't Kane's partner Hawes had killed. Let the chief struggle with whether his loyalty lay with the law or the Madigans. Chris knew where his lay: with Izzy. "ATF only."

With a sharp nod, Wheeler rose and hustled toward the door. "Give me an hour. I'll call in who I need and have a revised tactical ready—"

Chris waved him off. "Sleep, Scotty. We can go over everything in the morning. The op isn't until tomorrow night."

Wheeler let out a breath and a tired chuckle and ran a hand through his rumpled hair. "I broke up with sleep a long time ago."

"Kiss and make up," Chris said. "It's going to be a long day tomorrow. I need you sharp."

"I'll try. And you too."

He didn't give Chris a chance to respond or to pass back the list and photo in his hand. Chris stared at the missing pieces to the puzzle of that night three years ago. He was so close to bringing Izzy's killers to justice. He kept that thought at the front of his mind, ignoring the kernel of suspicion in the back of it that this—targeting Hawes and his siblings—was exactly what the person who'd engineered that night wanted him to do.

One hour and half a bottle of whisky later, that kernel of

doubt had turned into a whole field of corn. And Chris was fucking lost in it.

The confrontation with Hawes continued to play in his head, the *I'm Yours* no less loud. Nor was the image of a defiant yet resigned Hawes any less vivid. Shoulders square, jaw set, ready to take a bullet if Chris delivered it, tonight or a day from now.

Chris lifted the bottle of Crown Royal and took another swig. The fiery rye burned across his tongue and down his throat, but it failed to burn away the indecision that knotted his stomach, twisted his heart, and fucked with his head. Torn between what he wanted to do and what he should do, and the multiple options in each of those columns.

Fuck.

He capped the bottle and lay back on the narrow strip of grass he called a backyard, staring up at the dark sky that failed to give him any answers. He half expected Hawes to be lingering, to appear out of the fog at any moment, but so far, it was just Chris and the dark, unhelpful nothingness.

He closed his eyes, saw Hawes behind his lids, heard *I'm yours* in his ears, remembered Amelia's and Kane's words from the station, recalled Scotty's gleeful *King Slayer*, and the merry-go-round started again. Was he being manipulated too? Was he playing right into Reeves's hand? Did it fucking matter if he got justice for Izzy?

The spinning only stopped with the metal *clank* of the side-gate latch. Instantly alert, Chris rolled onto his side, adjusted his grip on the bottle, the only weapon he had at the ready, and cocked back his arm, preparing to hurl it at the late-night intruder. But then the burst of adrenaline sharpened into focus, and a tread as familiar as his own reached his ears.

Relaxing on his hip, he took another swig of whisky and waited for his sister to appear from around the corner. In the dark, with only the ambient light of the flat above them, the bruises on her face and neck weren't as glaring, but the way she moved was careful and measured, feeling the aches and pains of the fight with Dex. There was also a steely, encouraging set to her spine that had been long missing. And a helmet in her hands that made him grin. "You bring me a gift, Cee?"

"I brought you the thing that's required by law."

"You're such a mom."

"Shut it." She tossed her purse on the rusty, broken beach chair and lowered herself, cross-legged, next to him on the ground. "Lawyer called today. Wanted to say thank you."

"At midnight?"

"Another lawyer called. She said you might need someone tonight."

He raised a brow. "And you decided to be that person?"

She shoved the helmet at his chest, and he collapsed back, feigning injury. She laughed, a good, welcome sign, before snagging the bottle and taking a healthy swallow. "Neither of us has been there for the other like we should have been. Like we used to be. But you were there for me today, and I'm here for you now."

Warmth, the first since this morning, suffused his person and soothed a little of the ache in his chest, turned the chaos down a measure in his head. He ran a hand over the basic yet durable helmet, letting that calm him further too, thankful for the reprieve.

"You want to talk about it?" she asked.

"I found out who killed Izzy."

She covered his hand with hers. "Not the boyfriend?"

Fuck, he wished it had been Zander Rowe, wished he could rewind and tell the grief-stricken, vengeful Agent Perri of three years ago to let it go, to just accept the official cover version of events. It would have been a whole lot less painful, less complicated. "Not who I thought it was at all."

"And you're not happy about that."

He laughed, because what the fuck else was he going to do? Cry? He pushed himself upright, set the helmet on the ground, and reclaimed the bottle, taking another swig.

Gaze downcast, Celia picked at the shop grease under her nails. "Dex isn't who I thought he was either."

"Cee…"

"I know I have a blind spot where he's concerned, but we had some good years before the bad. He gave me two beautiful kids, but then he changed, and so did I." She sighed, heavy and tired. "But you know what didn't change? My responsibility to those kids, and I let them down. I should have left him years ago, for their sakes."

He'd seen the same play out before, in Jennifer's family and in the circles he'd infiltrated as an agent. He knew who was to blame, and it wasn't his sister or the kids. "That's not how abuse works, Cee."

"I'm not sure how a lot of things work."

"Except an engine."

She glanced up at him, a small, welcome smile flitting across her face. "That I do know."

"Dad taught us well. You better."

Surprising him, she reached for his hand. "But that's not the only engine he taught us about. Mom and Pop, they also showed us how to run the engine of a family and a job too. My kids, the shop, those are the things that keep me going. I'll focus on them, fine-tune 'em, and let that drive me. What's driving you, big brother?"

I'm yours.

He shook the thought away. "I'll sleep, then I'll get up tomorrow, and Special Agent Christopher Perri will do his job." One last time. For Izzy. For Ro. For this family. Complete his final mission and get out. He'd lost sight of that, blinded by a future he couldn't have. He remembered it now, and he'd let it drive him. He'd be done tomorrow, one way or the other.

EIGHTEEN

A black town car pulled into the drive of the Madigan family fort, headlights blasting the sage-green Victorian. Lights also beamed bright above, the house ablaze from the main floor all the way up to Holt's attic lair, giving the impression that the hacker was there. Not sitting behind Chris in the back seat of Kane's cruiser, parked in the shadows of the driveway across the street.

"Here we go," Helena singsonged, her voice echoing out of the cruiser's speakers. She leaned over and kissed Rose's cheek, the matriarch standing in front of the big bay windows, Lily in her arms.

"We've got you," Holt reported back as the red dot on the dashboard screen tracking Helena's movements headed for the door. "Keep your channel open so we can hear, but no further communication."

"Not a rook, Little H."

No, Helena definitely wasn't. Her posture was relaxed, her demeanor calm as she descended the porch steps, approached the town car, and stretched out her arms, allowing the driver to check her for weapons and devices. Unarmed and all clear, the same undetectable tech Chris had planted on Iris undetectable once more. The driver opened the door for her, and Helena slid into the back seat. She had no idea what she was getting into, who might be waiting for her, and yet the petite blonde clad in leather and cashmere didn't display an ounce of trepidation. Impressive was right, and confident in the fact that she was deadlier than a good percentage of the population.

Chris wondered, not for the first time since he'd squared off with her in Kane's office yesterday, how involved she'd been the night Izzy died. She'd clearly known what had happened and understood how the fallout had changed her brother. Had she been there? Had she left Izzy in the street? Been the one to tamper with the crime scene to make it look just enough like a domestic disturbance? With Kane then at SFPD, willing to cover for them, and the ATF silent, unwilling to disclose their presence, how much time and evidence had they lost? Maybe Chris would have put the pieces together sooner, before everything had become a jumbled mess.

"So, just me and you?" Helena's polite chitchat with the driver brought Chris back to the present. She was letting them know she was alone in the car as it started down the hill out of Pac Heights.

"Alpha on the move," Chris radioed the task force teams. "Tactical, hold for advance. Beta, go in sixty."

Exactly a minute later, a Benz crept out of the alley two blocks up, Avery behind the wheel, Hawes in the passenger seat. A blue dot appeared on Kane's dashboard screen, following a discreet distance behind the town car. "Beta on the move."

Kane waited another minute before easing the unmarked cruiser out after them. "Command on the move," Chris reported. "Tactical, hold another sixty, then commence advance."

As planned, Helena's response to the seller had insisted on visual proof. She wouldn't make any deal without clapping eyes on the entire lot of explosives. In reply, the seller proposed a meet, location undisclosed, making the task force's rolling tails one of the trickier aspects of the op. Never mind the twist Chris had planned for the end, assuming they secured the explosives first.

Toward that goal, they couldn't be seen before reaching the destination. The teams moved in a grid pattern behind them. Wheeler, at the tactical helm, called out the cross streets every few blocks, and the teams checked in, confirming their locations. There were additional teams in the field, positioned near the half dozen possible locations Chris and Wheeler had scouted, but none of them had reported any activity. As they continued down Third, across King, and past the ballpark and arena, Chris began to understand why, started to suspect where they were headed.

He swiveled in his seat. "Is this another fucking setup?"

Judging by the pale faces beside and behind him, he guessed not. Holt shook his head. "We weren't expecting this either."

Confirmed by Hawes's "Fucking hell" over the comm as the town car carrying their sister turned onto the road leading to the pier where MCS's headquarters were located. "We're following," Hawes said.

"Beta and Command only," Chris radioed the teams.

"Traffic is too light for all of us. Wheeler, shift the Hunter's Point tactical team to the pier here."

"On it," Wheeler said, then relayed the order down the line.

Chris tuned him out, trusting Scotty to do his job, and turned his attention to Hawes. "Do not go all the way to the gate, Madigan. Stealth approach. It's our best chance for salvaging this op."

"Fuck your op," Hawes practically growled. "I'm not letting my sister go in there alone. What part of trap don't you understand?"

He understood all of it, including the trap he had planned. He wasn't about to let this op go to shit either. "We devised a tactical plan for the pier down in Hunter's Point. We're shifting that team up here. By boat, they'll be here in ten minutes, max."

"Hena can stall at the gate," Holt said. "But that'll probably only buy us five minutes."

"Do it," Chris told him. "The other teams will get here in time for backup."

Holt relayed the request to Helena, who cleared her throat, signaling message received. Hawes smacked the dashboard of the Benz, clearly frustrated, a loud *thump* sounding over the comm. They'd boxed him in, hadn't given him an opportunity to object. He ordered Avery to pull into the parking lot a building over from MCS, and Kane swung the cruiser in beside them.

Hawes bolted out of the Benz and immediately took up his pacing. Sympathy sliced through Chris's chest—he'd be going crazy too if that were Celia—and his heart, as much as it hurt for Izzy, as much as it still stung from Hawes's betrayal, traitorously itched to comfort the other man.

He reverted to agent mode and shut his insides down, ignoring the irrepressible attraction and the lingering doubts that maybe he too was walking into a trap. Work the tactical; that was the best way to avoid it all. And the best way to get justice for Izzy. "Do you have staff on-site?" he asked Hawes.

"Minimal. We're between shifts at this time of night."

"Because someone knows exactly how you operate."

"Another fucking mole."

"Do we think the explosives are really there?" Kane asked.

Holt flashed the countdown clock on this tablet. "Four minutes left and we find out, one way or the other."

NINETEEN

Four minutes and Helena's expert stalling gave their small team time to converge on foot. Kane waited in the cruiser, prepared to run point as tactical arrived, while Chris, Hawes, Holt, and Avery approached via the adjacent property. Hawes picked the lock on their neighbor's gate, its fence behind the parking lot and closer to the building, unlike MCS's fully gated yard, and Holt hacked their alarm system, on the police chief's orders of course. It was a risk to have Holt here too, all the Madigan siblings on-site, but he'd refused to sit on the sidelines this time, and they needed him for exactly these situations. No one knew the security around here better. They snuck inside and crept along the shadowed walkway between the building and the barrier separating the two properties.

As they neared the back, where stairs led down to the docks and water, Chris drew their group to a halt and spoke in a whisper. "We'll be too exposed down on the dock."

"I'll go over first," Hawes said, pointing up at the barrier wall that descended in a set of terraced levels.

Chris gestured at the wall itself. "If there's a hostile on the other side, you gonna shoot 'em?"

Hawes's jaw hardened, his blue eyes shining bright with defiance. "I don't need a gun to take someone down."

"I know that," Chris replied, straining to keep his voice low and calm. "But we need every second we can get, and a quick, relatively silent takedown is necessary."

"I'll go over first." Avery held up her pistol, which was fitted with a silencer. "Lighter and quieter."

"No," Hawes said, voice brooking no argument. "We don't know who's on the other side of that wall. We can't shoot first and ask questions later. That's not how we work anymore."

Admiration surged in Chris's chest until he remembered why Hawes had those rules, and all that unbidden warmth froze in his veins. Hawes stared back at him, some of the hardness in his eyes softening with regret, making the same connection Chris had, but he still wasn't giving an inch.

Helena's voice cut through the stalemate. "You took my phone," she said to the driver. "If I had it, I could call our IT guy and find out what's up with this gate."

"Nice try," the driver replied. "What's the number? And no funny business. Just relay the problem."

She rattled off a string of digits, which when dialed, rang directly to Holt's comm. He answered, not letting on who he was, pretending instead to be a groggy IT guy just woken from sleep. She explained the issue, and he returned a, "Yes, Miss Madigan, give me just a minute." He clicked off the comm and turned to Chris. "Boost Hawes over on the count of three."

Now Chris was the one boxed in without a choice, Holt tapping away on his tablet as Hawes stepped closer. Close enough for his breath to tickle Chris's cheek, for the smell of expensive aftershave to tease his nose, for Hawes's heat to warm the chill that had overcome him a moment ago.

"One."

Hawes put a hand on Chris's shoulder, heat magnified tenfold, intensified by the vulnerable tremble in his grip that Hawes couldn't hide from him. Fuck but Chris hated that hesitation, hated this ebb and flow of trust and distrust between them. Hated that Hawes was right to doubt him. They had to trust each other, at least for the next hour, if any of them were going to get through this alive. And the bearing walls were there to do that. Yes, the foundation was shaky, both of them lying about pillars critical to the other, but they'd worked well together when they'd thought their interests were aligned.

"Two."

Chris sank into a crouch, hands cupped for Hawes's foot, and Hawes's grip on his shoulder tightened. Glancing up, Chris's eyes clashed with Hawes's, and a flood of memories washed over him like the waves lapping at the dock below. Chris in a similar position the night he sucked Hawes off against the ladder. Their positions reversed when Hawes had returned the favor in front of the couch. Their eyes locked in his reading nook, in the alley, as they'd been unable to resist each other this week, coming together again and again. Hawes trusting him. Chris had fallen for that heady gift, those blue eyes and the man they belonged to, his descent starting the second he'd walked into Danko the first time and spotted him across the room.

The man who'd killed his partner.

Fuck.

But was Hawes the same man? Nightmares of that night

plagued him, yet he got up every day and changed every-thing about himself, his life, and his organization so nothing like that night would happen again. To atone. For Izzy. To bring her justice.

Their interests were still aligned.

"Three."

Hawes put his foot in the cradle of Chris's hands and released his shoulder. Trusting him. Chris powered up and heaved the man who'd made a tangled mess of his insides, of his priorities over the wall.

A quiet *thump*, Hawes hitting the ground, was followed by a half-spoken, "Wha—" before the stranger's question was cut off. Two quick slaps of skin on skin, hand-to-hand combat, then another *thump*.

"Clear," Hawes said, and Chris didn't want to consider his relief at that single word in the king's familiar, confident tone. "Send Avery over, then come around the wall. We'll unlock the gate."

They gathered again outside the loading docks on the south side of the MCS facility. Hawes was shoving an unconscious merc clad in all black into a storage unit.

Chris had barely gotten out a, "Good work," when Helena's startled, "What the hell is going on here?" echoed over the comm.

"Exactly what was promised."

Chris's stomach sank, Holt hung his head, and Hawes cursed.

"Fuck," Avery gasped. "They got to Zoe too."

Another, deeper voice entered the fray, speaking to Helena. "A chance at the future."

Holt's head shot up. "Is that—"

"Carl Reeves," Hawes said.

Chris measured his reaction, not letting on that Reeves had recently shot to the top of his suspects list. It was a risk, surprising Hawes and the teams in the field, but Chris hadn't disclosed it in advance, not wanting to risk Hawes or anyone else eliminating his best chance at confirming the puppeteer behind Izzy's death. "Was he on Rose's list?" Chris asked.

Hawes shook his head. "We haven't done business with him in years. We wouldn't consider him a competitor in either business."

"Why'd you stop doing business with him?"

"Wasn't comfortable with how he was using our products and services."

That euphemism was almost as ironic as assassins running a cold storage business. "Seems he didn't take kindly to that."

"But he went his way, and we went ours," Holt said.

"Or," Chris ventured, "he's been circling like a shark this entire time."

Helena asked, "And if I don't accept?" drawing their attention back to the showdown happening in the front yard.

"I push this trigger, and the past is erased," Reeves replied. "The future moves on without you."

Chris's stomach went tumbling the rest of the way to his feet. "The explosives are here." He clicked over to Kane's open channel. "Chief, you hearing this?"

"Just gave the order to keep the teams back at the perimeter." He cleared his throat. "Get them out of there, Perri."

Chris clicked off without replying, hoping the excuse of Helena speaking again would be reason enough for his nonanswer. "You think Hawes will let that happen?" she said.

"We're not worried about the prince," Zoe said, notably not referring to him as king. "His days are numbered."

Hawes's gaze snapped to Chris, and the kernel of doubt in the back of Chris's head ballooned—burst—sending a chill snaking down his spine and out to his limbs. They were all being manipulated, moved around the board to satisfy Reeves.

"And Holt?" Helena asked.

"Will, in the end, do whatever it takes for those he loves."

Across from them, the man in question hung his head and laid a hand over his right pec, fingers digging into the flannel that covered a lotus tattoo in honor of his daughter. For a second, Chris thought they'd lost him, but Holt lifted his dark, determined eyes, then lifted them even farther, up toward the command perch on the top floor of the facility. "I'm going up," he said. "Depending on how they've wired the explosives, I might be able to do something about them from there."

Hawes nodded. "Avery, go with him."

They took off as Helena continued to stall, demanding proof of the explosives. Her gulp a moment later was audible. "You wired the north wing." Where all the manufacturing took place. "That's a fucking tinder box."

Reeves must have shown her a live feed on a tablet. Good. Better even if the trigger was on it, because then Holt had a chance. And in case he needed more time, Chris and Hawes needed to move. Chris gestured toward the standoff at the front of the building.

"Let's go," Hawes agreed, falling in behind him. "Hena, we're coming to you. Keep them talking."

She didn't miss a beat. "That's a stockpile's worth of explosives."

"All of them," Reeves said. "Mine now."

"If you blow it, you won't have any left."

"I've got recruits," Zoe said, and by the shuffling of gravel behind them, she had a good many there on-site with them. "Soldiers who've done the dirty work, making and exploding them for years. They'll make more for us. We're not afraid to sell and use them."

"And the display will be powerful," Reeves added. "You should be a part of it."

"Why would I join you?"

"Why wouldn't you? There's nothing holding you to your current life. You could still live your life and do your job if you need to. We wouldn't care."

We. Was he referring to Zoe or someone else?

"She said you were the star, an asset the organization couldn't lose."

She.

"*Amelia*?" Hawes mouthed, brow raised.

Chris was likewise skeptical and mentally ticked through the options. From questioning Amelia, Chris didn't think she was the sort to heap praise on Helena. Zoe, while in the inner circle, didn't ever strike Chris as having that kind of worship for Amelia either. But Avery…

Pale-faced, Hawes had already reached the same conclusion and turned his gaze skyward, looking up toward his brother's office. It was dark, no sign of movement, but Holt would know not to turn the lights on, to operate under the radar as long as possible.

Wouldn't he?

If he ever made it up there.

Holt down wasn't necessarily contrary to Chris's objective, but fuck, he did not want the younger twin, who really would do anything for those he loved, his daughter especially, to go out that way. It was too cruel a fate for Lily and those who loved him, including Hawes.

"We're set." Holt's voice came over the comm, and both Chris and Hawes gasped out a held breath. "I'm tapped into their signal."

"Take these fuckers down," Avery added, proving her loyalty once more.

Hawes grinned, that wicked, beautiful thing that made Chris's blood run piping-hot and knotted his insides. He shouldn't want it, shouldn't want him, but he was irresistible. And that picture of home that had been shifting in Chris's head? It included this Hawes, the man he was now. The emptiness Chris felt after the auction, after almost losing him, knowing if he had lost him the puzzle would be incomplete, was proof enough.

I'm yours. And he was Hawes's.

And their common objectives—the explosives and the seller, and the person who may have set Izzy up to die, who may have set up Hawes to pull the trigger—were in their grasp.

Chris crept toward the corner of the building and fought off a full body shiver when Hawes put a steady hand to his lower back, no more trembling, trusting now, braced to enter the war with him.

"You forgot one thing," Helena said. "I'm loyal."

"To your family," Zoe said.

"Exactly. To my brothers."

"All teams, hold at the perimeter," Kane ordered over the comm. "Be prepared to go when the lights come up."

"You'll die for that loyalty," Reeves said, and pressed the button on the trigger.

Brightness exploded, but not from the bombs—from every light in and around the facility suddenly blazing to life.

The battle was on, and Chris and Hawes entered it, together.

For a few valuable seconds, everyone in the yard stood frozen, blinded by the lights and waiting for the blast that never came. It was the opening Chris and Hawes needed to bolt from behind the building and reach Helena, who expertly handled the Ka-Bar Hawes tossed her direction. It hit her palm with a *smack*, and it was like pressing Play on a recording. Everything around them snapped back into action.

At Zoe's signal, three soldiers rushed them. Chris introduced one to his boot, kicking clear his weapon. Momentum carrying him, he planted his kicking leg and swung the other around, delivering a round house kick to the soldier's head. The soldier crumpled in an unconscious heap.

"No promotion for that one," Hawes said, as he yanked back another soldier's elbows with his garrote, the angle unnatural, the *crack* of bones sickening. "No promotion for this one either." With a smooth flick of the wrist, Hawes withdrew the wire and the soldier's broken arms fell limp. Hawes kicked him in the kidneys and sent him flying face first into the pavement.

They turned in unison to Helena. Her back was to them, her knife dripping blood onto the downed soldier at her feet. He was breathing still but decorated in blooming red slash marks. "That all you got, traitor," Helena hollered at Zoe.

Hawes spoke to the other soldiers. "They've fooled you. Lay your weapons down and no retribution will come to you."

"Like Lucas, Jodie, and Ray?" Zoe countered.

"They made their decisions," Hawes replied. "Now I'm giving these soldiers the same choice."

Several fell back, but an equal number remained at Zoe's side. She didn't, however, send them in the next wave of attack. Mercs were more expendable than valuable soldiers. No shots were fired. They'd clearly been given the order to capture, not kill. Chris went hand to hand with one, and out of the corner of his eye, watched as Hawes and Helena worked in perfect tandem. Catch, slice, release. None fatal, but those hired guns weren't getting back up anytime soon. Neither was the merc Chris finally choked out with his denim jacket.

Helena looked on approvingly. "Double denim for the win."

The reprieve was short-lived, and Chris worried the next, larger wave of attack would be more than their trio could handle. Hawes recognized it too. He stepped closer, their shoulders brushing. "She's trying to wear us out."

"Call in the captains?" Helena said.

"No," Hawes said. "We need them in reserve."

"No need," Holt radioed. "Rest of the cavalry is here."

He'd barely finished speaking when the flash of blue and red lights reflected in the charging mercenaries' eyes.

"Break, Hena!" Hawes shouted.

She spun left, Hawes right, taking Chris with him. The maneuver put them outside the mercs charging into the middle, easier to handle just the few on the perimeter, while the others scattered in the wake of cop cars and cruisers setting up a barricade, officers and agents taking position behind them.

"We brought friends!" Hawes said.

"Cops and feds," Reeves said. "What happened to you?"

"I trusted the right people."

Warmth flooded Chris's chest, then fled at Reeves's next words. "They'll find the explosives and arrest you."

That had been the plan, but Chris had thrown that plan into jeopardy when he'd thrown Hawes over that wall. Tossed it out all together when Hawes had laid a hand on his back as they'd prepared to charge the yard. Together. At least for the duration of this battle. Longer, if he could figure out how to reconcile justice, his conscience, and his heart. He didn't think the answer in any scenario was the arrest or death of Hawes Madigan or his siblings.

As for the immediate challenge, Holt solved that problem for them. Zoe's and Reeves's own pre-battle words —claiming ownership of the explosives, the intent to make, sell, and use more—blasted out of the yard speakers.

"Sounds like those are your weapons," Hawes said.

"Which you intend to use in the commission of a crime," Chris added.

"With the intent to make and distribute more," Helena

finished. "And you can bet we'll also be filing trespassing charges."

"And the bodies at your feet?" Reeves said.

"Not dead," Chris replied. "And if they were, self-defense." Beside him, Hawes chuckled. Chris likewise smiled at the irony of his words, the past week coming full circle.

"Stand down, Reeves," Kane bellowed through a megaphone. "It's over."

"Fall back!" Zoe ordered. Only two soldiers joined her and Reeves and the couple remaining mercs as they sprinted around the opposite side of the building and down the access ramp to the water.

"They're headed for the docks!" Hawes said.

"They'll run into agents that way," Chris said. The boat coming up from Hunter's Point, and Wheeler's three-man team who thought they were there to capture Hawes.

"I'll stay and manage the scene here," Helena said. "Go!"

Rather than following down the ramp, Hawes ran flat-out toward the front door, Chris in his wake. "We'll go through the middle," he said, as the doors opened for them. "Thanks, Little H."

They circled the security desk, cut through the break room and cafeteria, and hustled down the same stairwell they'd used last week. Hawes slammed open the emergency exit door to a hail of gunfire, and Chris acted on instinct, forcing him against the wall and covering Hawes's body with his larger one. Hawes could be pissed at him later.

Except he wasn't. He fisted the sides of Chris's shirt and held him tighter, closer, face buried in the crook of his neck.

"You hit?" Chris whispered in his ear. Hawes shook his head. Neither was Chris. He looked up and around. They were alone. Gunfire broke out again. "It's at the docks."

Hawes drew back enough to meet his gaze. "I'm sorry. I just needed a second."

Chris lowered an arm from over Hawes's head and palmed his cheek. "Steady, now?"

He nodded, confident once more. "Let's go."

Chris, however, held him firm. There was one more thing he needed to say, before they walked into the firefight. "You need to know—"

"That you intended to arrest me, if we survived this night."

Chris blinked, then smiled. Of course he knew. "That's not my intention anymore."

Hawes circled his wrist, fingers over his pulse point, and squeezed. "My promise holds. I'm yours, either way."

Chris knew which of the options he wanted now. But the ratcheting up of gunfire drew their attention and they were off again, running for the docks. The scene there was not good. Wheeler's team of ATF agents, plus the four-man team from the other boat, were now on Gilbert's salvage vessel, taking on Zoe, Reeves and their reinforcements. It should have been an easy win for the ATF, based on numbers, but while their orders were to capture, the bad guys had no qualms about killing or throwing LEOs overboard.

Zoe was directly engaged with Wheeler while Reeves and Gilbert stood out of the way by the helm, like this was not what they'd signed up for. Chris thought maybe they could use that. He and Hawes crept closer, almost to the boat. The view was good enough, the distance short enough, that when Zoe pulled her gun and shot Scotty in the side, right where the Kevlar didn't cover, she caught Chris's movement as his hand whipped to his side arm.

"Came to play, finally."

"Zoe, let's go!" Reeves yelled.

"He's not the one pulling the strings," Chris said under his breath.

As Chris made the observation, Zoe swung her gun arm around and shot Reeves, point-blank between the eyes. Gilbert screamed, which was the exact wrong move. Zoe's focus shifted to him, and he went down in a heap next to Reeves.

Her attention diverted, Hawes made a break for the boat. Cursing, Chris drew his weapon and ran after him. They got two steps onto the deck when Zoe brought them up short with a warning shot right between their heads.

"Reeves fits your criteria," she said to Hawes. "The smuggler too. Don't they?"

Hawes didn't take the bait. "Who are you working for?"

"The person who's always put this organization's interests first."

"You calling working with Reeves putting us first?"

"He was a pawn, like all of you." Her hazel gaze shifted to Chris. "Including your old partner. She knew."

Chris gasped. "What?" His knees would have given out from under him, if he hadn't stood braced against the waves already.

Zoe smirked, the same smug grin that Tamela had worn at the BART station. "So does your current partner. He came to us, just like Isabella did. But I'm done trusting feds."

She raised her arm, gun pointed directly at Scotty's

head, and Chris didn't hesitate to draw his and fire. At Zoe. She crumpled to the deck, lifeless, and Hawes crumpled over, hands on his knees, expelling a giant breath.

Chris's head was spinning with the revelations of the past minute, but he kept himself upright by focusing on the man beside him, who was reining in what had to be an even bigger hurricane in his mind. He laid a hand on Hawes's back and circled to kneel in front of him. "She was going to kill him."

Eyes still closed, Hawes nodded. "It was the right move. The last thing we need are more dead feds."

So much for ignoring Zoe's words about Izzy. Was the lieutenant playing them? Or was there more to the story of Izzy's murder than Chris or Hawes knew? Chris was ninety-nine percent sure Izzy hadn't been dirty, but he couldn't say that with one hundred percent certainty. Tran believed she'd gone rogue when she'd gone dark right before her death. Chris didn't have an explanation for it, and now there were more questions swirling in that dark space. Questions that made him hold back that one percent. A one percent they needed to account for, and the person who could help them get answers—the person Chris had zero doubts about—was on this boat.

"Listen to me, Hawes." Blue eyes opened and locked onto his. "Scotty Wheeler is the last person—"

"I believe you." Hawes took a deep breath and straightened, and Chris moved to check on Scotty.

The agent was still breathing, and the blood loss was thankfully slow. The hit to his head when he'd fallen was probably what had knocked him out. Chris grabbed a deck towel, shoved it over the wound, and rearranged Scotty's vest to keep the towel wedged there.

"Got a tip earlier today that he was dirty," Hawes said. "More traps."

Chris stood and looked back and forth between him and Wheeler. "Then—"

"She needs to think I fell for it. And I need you to help me sell it."

Anger sparked brightest in the whirlwind of emotions, all of it spinning too fast. "What part of don't leave me out of the loop—"

Hawes cut him off and deflated his anger by stepping forward and putting one hand on his hip and the other around his neck. "Until twenty minutes ago, I thought you were going to kill me, not kill to protect my organization."

Chris closed the distance between them and rested his forehead against Hawes's. "Baby, I can't kill you. I think I might love you."

Hawes inhaled sharply, then smiled that wry grin that twisted and warmed Chris's insides. "Will you still love me when I throw you off this boat?"

"Fuck, I was afraid of that." He stepped back and looked over the side at the dark water, all thoughts of warmth fleeing. He couldn't look at Hawes when he asked, "Do you know who she is?" He didn't want to see the hurt in his eyes, didn't think he could bear it.

"I think so, and I think you do too. I can't believe my—" The hurt in his voice, though, was a million times worse.

Turning back to him, Chris put a hand over his mouth to stop the painful sound. "Don't say it, not until you're sure." He nodded at Wheeler. "I had my suspicions too. Had him check. That's probably why they flagged him, then tried to get you to eliminate him."

"Two birds, one stone."

"Same as they tried the night of Izzy's murder." Which was a thousand times more complicated now. "When he comes to, he's your best bet for confirming it. And Izzy's involvement."

"*If* she was involved."

Chris appreciated the consideration, what it meant that Hawes was willing to hold on to Izzy's innocence, and in doing so, his own culpability in her death. It spoke to the man he was, the man Chris had fallen for. The man who deserved his consideration. "We need to find out the whole truth." He glanced again at Scotty and sent up a prayer for forgiveness for tangling him up in all this. "Protect him."

"You know I will." Hawes ran a shaking hand through his hair, glancing back up the hill where shouts were growing louder and flashlight beams brighter. Kane and his men weren't around the corner yet, but any minute now… "If we're right, I may have to bend the knee."

Chris grabbed his hand and laced their fingers, hauling Hawes close once more. "We've been fighting this from the outside. We fight from the inside, if we have to. That might be the only way we find the truth."

"All of it," Hawes said, some of his confidence returning.

"All of it," Chris repeated, then shoved the butt of his gun in Hawes's middle, same as Hawes had done to him last night. "Sell it, either way." Chris swallowed Hawes's gasp, pouring everything into the kiss—admiration, love, trust—and getting the trust back that he so desperately needed. The trust that they would need to find their way home again, because that's what Hawes was to him. Undeniably. The picture was clear.

Gun in hand, Hawes drew back with a final, achingly

sweet kiss to the corner of his mouth. "I think I might love you too."

Warmth flooded Chris from the center of his chest out to his fingers and toes, shielding him from the pain of the bullet that ripped through his shoulder and the cold dark water of the Bay that swallowed him whole.

Don't stop now!
Hawes & Chris's story reaches its exciting romantic conclusion in *A New Empire*!

For all the latest updates on new projects, sneak peeks, and more, sign up for Layla's Newsletter.

Reviews are an invaluable tool when it comes to spreading the word about great reads. Please consider leaving an honest review for *King Slayer* on your favorite review site.

Thank you for reading!

ACKNOWLEDGMENTS

First and foremost, thank you Readers, especially my Lushes, for the continued enthusiasm for this series and all my books. Your support and love of my stories truly mean the world to me!

Thank you to the team that makes *Fog City* shine: Wander Aguiar and models Patrick and Ryan for the piping hot photography, Cate Ashwood for another amazing cover, Kristi Yanta for always being a phone call or text away when I need a story check-in, Keren Reed for the copy editing expertise, Susan Selva for being the best pair of eyes on my words, and Leslie Copeland for beta reading the first draft and assembling the last one. Speaking of betas, my thanks, love, and all the caffeine to Erin, Lisa, Allison, and Kim for pushing me through this one with their cheering and insightful feedback. Thanks to Judith and the ANTPR team for spreading the word, and thank you Tantor Audio and the incomparable Tristan James for bringing this world to life for listeners!

Thank you again to all the wonderful authors and friends who continue to be an invaluable support system as I swim deeper into these self-pub waters. And thank you to my agent, Laura Bradford, for throwing out a life preserver when I needed it most.

ALSO BY LAYLA REYNE

For the most up-to-date list of titles and a helpful reading order, please visit www.laylareyne.com.

Agents Irish and Whiskey:

Single Malt

Cask Strength

Barrel Proof

Tequila Sunrise

Blended Whiskey

Angel's Share

Trouble Brewing:

Imperial Stout

Craft Brew

Noble Hops

Final Gravity

Fog City:

Prince of Killers

King Slayer

A New Empire

Queen's Ransom

Silent Knight

Perfect Play:

Dead Draw

Bad Bishop

King Hunt

Best Play

Redemption Inc.:

The Accidental

The Bounty

The Martyr

The Boss

More Romantic Suspense / Mystery:

What We May Be

Variable Onset

Soul to Find:

Icarus and the Devil

Jason and the Storm

Paris and the Reaper

Atlas and the Traitor

Table for Two:

The Last Drop

Dine With Me

Blue Plate Special

Over a Barrel

The Sweet Spot

Sigh of Relief

ABOUT THE AUTHOR

Layla Reyne is the author of *What We May Be* and the *Agents Irish and Whiskey, Fog City,* and *Perfect Play* series. She writes sexy, intense LGBTQIA+ romance featuring competent adults in kitchens, sports arenas, car chases, and other high-stakes situations. Whether it's adrenaline-fueled suspense, rival athletes, vampires and shifters, or love mixed with mouth-watering foodie goodness, queer folks finding happily-ever-afters is guaranteed.

You can find Layla online at laylareyne.com and at the following sites:

BB   bookbub.com/authors/layla-reyne

f   facebook.com/laylareyne

instagram.com/laylareyne

tiktok.com/@laylareyne

bsky.app/profile/laylareyne